FREE JOE

AND

OTHER GEORGIAN SKETCHES

FREE JOE

AND

OTHER GEORGIAN SKETCHES

BY

JOEL CHANDLER HARRIS

AUTHOR OF "UNCLE REMUS," ETC., ETC.

THE GREGG PRESS / RIDGEWOOD, N. J.

First published in 1887 by Charles Scribner's Sons
Republished in 1967 by
The Gregg Press Incorporated
171 East Ridgewood Avenue
Ridgewood, New Jersey, U.S.A.
Copyright © 1967 by
The Gregg Press, Inc.

Library of Congress Catalog Card Number: 67-29268

Printed in United States of America

AMERICANS
IN
FICTION

INTRODUCTION BY PROFESSOR CLARENCE GOHDES
Editor of *American Literature* Magazine

In the domain of literature the play may once have been the chief abstract and chronicle of the times, but during the nineteenth and twentieth centuries the novel has usurped the chief place in holding the mirror up to the homely face of society. On this account, if for no other, the Gregg Press series of reprints of American fiction merits the attention of all students of Americana and of librarians interested in building up adequate collections dealing with the social and literary history of the United States. Most of the three score and ten novels or volumes of short stories included in the series enjoyed considerable fame in their day but have been so long out of print as to be virtually unobtainable in the original editions.

Included in the list are works by writers not presently fashionable in critical circles — but nevertheless well known to literary historians — among them Joel Chandler Harris, Harriet Beecher Stowe, Thomas Bailey Aldrich, and William Gilmore Simms. A substantial element in the list consists of authors who are known especially for their graphic portrayal of a particular American setting, such as Gertrude Atherton (California), Arlo Bates (Boston), Alice Brown (New England), Edward Eggleston (Indiana), Mary Wilkins Freeman (New England), Henry B. Fuller (Chicago), Richard M. Johnston (Georgia), James Lane Allen (Kentucky), Mary N. Murfree (Tennessee), and Thomas Nelson Page (Virginia). There is even a novel by Frederic Remington, one of the most popular painters of the Western cowboy and Indian — and another, an impressive minor classic on the early mining region of Colorado, from the pen of Mary Hallock Foote. The professional student of American literature will rejoice in the opportunity afforded by the collection to extend his reading of fiction belonging to what is called the "local-color movement" — a major current in the development of the national belles-lettres.

Among the titles in the series are also a number of famous historical novels. Silas Weir Mitchell's *Hugh Wynne* is one of the best fictional treatments of the American Revolution. John Esten Cooke is the foremost Southern writer of his day who dealt with the Civil War. The two books by Thomas Dixon are among the most famous novels on the Reconstruction Era, with sensational disclosures of the original Ku Klux Klan in action. They supplied the grist for the first great movie "spectacular" — *"The Birth of a Nation* (1915).

Paul Leicester Ford's *The Honorable Peter Stirling* is justly ranked among the top American novels which portray American politics in action — a subject illuminated by other novelists in the Gregg list — A. H. Lewis, Frances H. Burnett, and Alice Brown, for example. Economic problems are forcefully put before the reader in works by Aldrich, Mrs. Freeman, and John Hay, whose novels illustrate the ominous concern over the early battles between labor and capital. From the sweatshops of Eastern cities in which newly arrived immigrants toiled for pittances, to the Western mining camps where the laborers packed revolvers, the working class of the times enters into various other stories in the Gregg list. The capitalist class, also, comes in for attention, with an account of a struggle for the ownership of a railroad in Samuel Merwin's *The Short-Line War* and with the devastating documentation of the foibles of the newly rich and their wives in the narratives of David Graham Phillips. It was Phillips whose annoying talent for the exposure of abuses led Theodore Roosevelt to put the term "muck-raker" into currency.

While it is apparent that local-color stories, the historical novel, and the economic novel have all been borne in mind in choosing the titles for this important series of reprints, it is evident that careful consideration has also been given to treatments of various minority elements in the American population. The Negro, especially, but also the Indian, the half-breed, Creoles, Cajuns — and even the West Coast Japanese — appear as characters in various of these novels or volumes of short stories and sketches. Joel Chandler Harris's *Free Joe* will open the eyes of readers who know that author solely as the creator of humorous old Uncle Remus. And there is a revelatory volume of dialect tales, written by a Negro author, *The Conjure Woman* by Charles W. Chesnutt.

In literary conventions and the dominating attitudes toward life, the works in the Gregg series range from the adventurous romance illustrated so well by Mayne Reid or the polite urbanity of Owen Wister to the mordant irony of Kate Chopin and the grimmer realism of Joseph Kirkland's own experiences on bloody Civil War battlefields or the depressing display of New York farm life by Harold Frederic. In short, the series admirably illustrates the general qualities of the fiction produced in the United States during the era covered, just as it generously mirrors the geographical regions, the people, and the problems of the times.

CONTENTS.

FREE JOE AND THE REST OF THE WORLD.

THE name of Free Joe strikes humorously upon the ear of memory. It is impossible to say why, for he was the humblest, the simplest, and the most serious of all God's living creatures, sadly lacking in all those elements that suggest the humorous. It is certain, moreover, that in 1850 the sober-minded citizens of the little Georgian village of Hillsborough were not inclined to take a humorous view of Free Joe, and neither his name nor his presence provoked a smile. He was a black atom, drifting hither and thither without an owner, blown about by all the winds of circumstance, and given over to shiftlessness.

The problems of one generation are the paradoxes of a succeeding one, particularly if war, or some such incident, intervenes to clarify the atmosphere and strengthen the understanding. Thus, in 1850, Free Joe represented not only a problem of large concern, but, in the watchful eyes of Hillsborough, he was the embodiment of that vague and mysterious danger that seemed to be forever lurking on the outskirts of slavery, ready to sound a shrill and ghostly

signal in the impenetrable swamps, and steal forth
under the midnight stars to murder, rapine, and pillage, — a danger always threatening, and yet never
assuming shape ; intangible, and yet real ; impossible, and yet not improbable. Across the serene and
smiling front of safety, the pale outlines of the awful
shadow of insurrection sometimes fell. With this
invisible panorama as a background, it was natural
that the figure of Free Joe, simple and humble as it
was, should assume undue proportions. Go where
he would, do what he might, he could not escape the
finger of observation and the kindling eye of suspicion. His lightest words were noted, his slightest
actions marked.

Under all the circumstances it was natural that his
peculiar condition should reflect itself in his habits
and manners. The slaves laughed loudly day by
day, but Free Joe rarely laughed. The slaves sang
at their work and danced at their frolics, but no one
ever heard Free Joe sing or saw him dance. There
was something painfully plaintive and appealing in
his attitude, something touching in his anxiety to
please. He was of the friendliest nature, and seemed
to be delighted when he could amuse the little children who had made a playground of the public
square. At times he would please them by making
his little dog Dan perform all sorts of curious tricks,
or he would tell them quaint stories of the beasts of
the field and birds of the air ; and frequently he was

coaxed into relating the story of his own freedom. That story was brief, but tragical.

In the year of our Lord 1840, when a negro-specu-lator of a sportive turn of mind reached the little village of Hillsborough on his way to the Mississippi region, with a caravan of likely negroes of both sexes, he found much to interest him. In that day and at that time there were a number of young men in the village who had not bound themselves over to repentance for the various misdeeds of the flesh. To these young men the negro-speculator (Major Framp-ton was his name) proceeded to address himself. He was a Virginian, he declared; and, to prove the statement, he referred all the festively inclined young men of Hillsborough to a barrel of peach-brandy in one of his covered wagons. In the minds of these young men there was less doubt in regard to the age and quality of the brandy than there was in regard to the negro-trader's birthplace. Major Frampton might or might not have been born in the Old Dominion, — that was a matter for consideration and inquiry, — but there could be no question as to the mellow pungency of the peach-brandy.

In his own estimation, Major Frampton was one of the most accomplished of men. He had summered at the Virginia Springs; he had been to Philadelphia, to Washington, to Richmond, to Lynchburg, and to Charleston, and had accumulated a great deal of ex-perience which he found useful. Hillsborough was hid in the woods of Middle Georgia, and its general aspect of innocence impressed him. He looked on the young men who had shown their readiness to test his peach-brandy, as overgrown country boys who needed to be introduced to some of the arts and sciences he had at his command. Thereupon the major pitched his tents, figuratively speaking, and became, for the time being, a part and parcel of the innocence that characterized Hillsborough. A wiser man would doubtless have made the same mistake.

The little village possessed advantages that seemed to be providentially arranged to fit the various enterprises that Major Frampton had in view. There was the auction-block in front of the stuccoed court-house, if he desired to dispose of a few of his negroes; there was a quarter-track, laid out to his hand and in excellent order, if he chose to enjoy the pleasures of horse-racing; there were secluded pine thickets within easy reach, if he desired to indulge in the exciting pastime of cock-fighting; and various lonely and unoccupied rooms in the second story of the tavern, if he cared to challenge the chances of dice or cards.

Major Frampton tried them all with varying luck, until he began his famous game of poker with Judge Alfred Wellington, a stately gentleman with a flowing white beard and mild blue eyes that gave him the appearance of a benevolent patriarch. The history of the game in which Major Frampton and Judge Alfred

Wellington took part is something more than a tradition in Hillsborough, for there are still living three
or four men who sat around the table and watched
its progress. It is said that at various stages of the
game Major Frampton would destroy the cards with
which they were playing, and send for a new pack,
but the result was always the same. The mild blue
eyes of Judge Wellington, with few exceptions, continued to overlook "hands" that were invincible —
a habit they had acquired during a long and arduous
course of training from Saratoga to New Orleans.
Major Frampton lost his money, his horses, his
wagons, and all his negroes but one, his body-servant. When his misfortune had reached this limit,
the major adjourned the game. The sun was shining
brightly, and all nature was cheerful. It is said that
the major also seemed to be cheerful. However this
may be, he visited the court-house, and executed the
papers that gave his body-servant his freedom. This
being done, Major Frampton sauntered into a convenient pine thicket, and blew out his brains.

The negro thus freed came to be known as Free
Joe. Compelled, under the law, to choose a guard-
ian, he chose Judge Wellington, chiefly because his
wife Lucinda was among the negroes won from
Major Frampton. For several years Free Joe had
what may be called a jovial time. His wife Lucinda
was well provided for, and he found it a comparatively easy matter to provide for himself; so that,

taking all the circumstances into consideration, it is not matter for astonishment that he became somewhat shiftless.

When Judge Wellington died, Free Joe's troubles began. The judge's negroes, including Lucinda, went to his half-brother, a man named Calderwood, who was a hard master and a rough customer generally, — a man of many eccentricities of mind and character. His neighbors had a habit of alluding to him as "Old Spite;" and the name seemed to fit him so completely, that he was known far and near as "Spite" Calderwood. He probably enjoyed the distinction the name gave him; at any rate, he never resented it, and it was not often that he missed an opportunity to show that he deserved it. Calderwood's place was two or three miles from the village of Hillsborough, and Free Joe visited his wife twice a week, Wednesday and Saturday nights.

One Sunday he was sitting in front of Lucinda's cabin, when Calderwood happened to pass that way.

"Howdy, marster?" said Free Joe, taking off his hat.

"Who are you?" exclaimed Calderwood abruptly, halting and staring at the negro.

"I'm name' Joe, marster. I'm Lucindy's ole man."

"Who do you belong to?"

"Marse John Evans is my gyardeen, marster."

"Big name — gyardeen. Show your pass."

Free Joe produced that document, and Calderwood read it aloud slowly, as if he found it difficult to get at the meaning : —

"*To whom it may concern : This is to certify that the boy Joe Frampton has my permission to visit his wife Lucinda.*"

This was dated at Hillsborough, and signed "*John W. Evans.*"

Calderwood read it twice, and then looked at Free Joe, elevating his eyebrows, and showing his discolored teeth.

"Some mighty big words in that there. Evans owns this place, I reckon. When's he comin' down to take hold ?"

Free Joe fumbled with his hat. He was badly frightened.

"Lucindy say she speck you wouldn't min' my comin', long ez I behave, marster."

Calderwood tore the pass in pieces and flung it away.

"Don't want no free niggers 'round here," he exclaimed. "There's the big road. It'll carry you to town. Don't let me catch you here no more. Now, mind what I tell you."

Free Joe presented a shabby spectacle as he moved off with his little dog Dan slinking at his heels. It should be said in behalf of Dan, however, that his bristles were up, and that he looked back and growled. It may be that the dog had the advantage

of insignificance, but it is difficult to conceive how a
dog bold enough to raise his bristles under Calderwood's very eyes could be as insignificant as Free
Joe. But both the negro and his little dog seemed
to give a new and more dismal aspect to forlornness
as they turned into the road and went toward Hillsborough.

After this incident Free Joe appeared to have
clearer ideas concerning his peculiar condition. He
realized the fact that though he was free he was
more helpless than any slave. Having no owner,
every man was his master. He knew that he was
the object of suspicion, and therefore all his slender
resources (ah! how pitifully slender they were!)
were devoted to winning, not kindness and appreciation, but toleration ; all his efforts were in the direction of mitigating the circumstances that tended to
make his condition so much worse than that of the
negroes around him, — negroes who had friends
because they had masters.

So far as his own race was concerned, Free Joe
was an exile. If the slaves secretly envied him his
freedom (which is to be doubted, considering his miserable condition), they openly despised him, and lost
no opportunity to treat him with contumely. Perhaps this was in some measure the result of the attitude which Free Joe chose to maintain toward them.
No doubt his instinct taught him that to hold himself aloof from the slaves would be to invite from the

whites the toleration which he coveted, and without which even his miserable condition would be rendered more miserable still.

His greatest trouble was the fact that he was not allowed to visit his wife; but he soon found a way out of this difficulty. After he had been ordered away from the Calderwood place, he was in the habit of wandering as far in that direction as prudence would permit. Near the Calderwood place, but not on Calderwood's land, lived an old man named Micajah Staley and his sister Becky Staley. These people were old and very poor. Old Micajah had a palsied arm and hand; but, in spite of this, he managed to earn a precarious living with his turning-lathe.

When he was a slave Free Joe would have scorned these representatives of a class known as poor white trash, but now he found them sympathetic and helpful in various ways. From the back door of their cabin he could hear the Calderwood negroes singing at night, and he sometimes fancied he could distinguish Lucinda's shrill treble rising above the other voices. A large poplar grew in the woods some distance from the Staley cabin, and at the foot of this tree Free Joe would sit for hours with his face turned toward Calderwood's. His little dog Dan would curl up in the leaves near by, and the two seemed to be as comfortable as possible.

One Saturday afternoon Free Joe, sitting at the foot of this friendly poplar, fell asleep. How long

he slept, he could not tell ; but when he awoke little
Dan was licking his face, the moon was shining
brightly, and Lucinda his wife stood before him
laughing. The dog, seeing that Free Joe was asleep,
had grown somewhat impatient, and he concluded to
make an excursion to the Calderwood place on his
own account. Lucinda was inclined to give the
incident a twist in the direction of superstition.

"I 'uz settin' down front er de fireplace," she said,
"cookin' me some meat, w'en all of a sudden I year
sumpin at de do' — scratch, scratch. I tuck'n tu'n
de meat over, en make out I aint year it. Bimeby it
come dar 'gin — scratch, scratch. I up en open de
do', I did, en, bless de Lord! dar wuz little Dan, en
it look like ter me dat his ribs donc grow tergeer.
I gin 'im some bread, en den, w'en he start out, I
tuck'n foller 'im, kaze, I say ter myse'f, maybe my
nigger man mought be some'rs 'roun'. Dat ar little
dog got sense, mon."

Free Joe laughed and dropped his hand lightly on
Dan's head. For a long time after that he had no
difficulty in seeing his wife. He had only to sit by
the poplar-tree until little Dan could run and fetch
her. But after a while the other negroes discovered
that Lucinda was meeting Free Joe in the woods,
and information of the fact soon reached Calderwood's ears. Calderwood was what is called a man
of action. He said nothing; but one day he put
Lucinda in his buggy, and carried her to Macon, sixty

miles away. He carried her to Macon, and came back without her; and nobody in or around Hillsborough, or in that section, ever saw her again.

For many a night after that Free Joe sat in the woods and waited. Little Dan would run merrily off and be gone a long time, but he always came back without Lucinda. This happened over and over again. The "willis-whistlers" would call and call, like phantom huntsmen wandering on a far-off shore; the screech-owl would shake and shiver in the depths of the woods; the night-hawks, sweeping by on noiseless wings, would snap their beaks as though they enjoyed the huge joke of which Free Joe and little Dan were the victims; and the whip-poor-wills would cry to each other through the gloom. Each night seemed to be lonelier than the preceding, but Free Joe's patience was proof against loneliness. There came a time, however, when little Dan refused to go after Lucinda. When Free Joe motioned him in the direction of the Calderwood place, he would simply move about uneasily and whine; then he would curl up in the leaves and make himself comfortable.

One night, instead of going to the poplar-tree to wait for Lucinda, Free Joe went to the Staley cabin, and, in order to make his welcome good, as he expressed it, he carried with him an armful of fat-pine splinters. Miss Becky Staley had a great reputation in those parts as a fortune-teller, and the schoolgirls,

as well as older people, often tested her powers in
this direction, some in jest and some in earnest.
Free Joe placed his humble offering of light-wood in
the chimney-corner, and then seated himself on the
steps, dropping his hat on the ground outside.

"Miss Becky," he said presently, "whar in de
name er gracious you reckon Lucindy is?"

"Well, the Lord he'p the nigger!" exclaimed Miss
Becky, in a tone that seemed to reproduce, by some
curious agreement of sight with sound, her general
aspect of peakedness. "Well, the Lord he'p the
nigger! haint you been a-seein' her all this blessed
time? She's over at old Spite Calderwood's, if she's
anywheres, I reckon."

"No'm, dat I aint, Miss Becky. I aint seen
Lucindy in now gwine on mighty nigh a mont'."

"Well, it haint a-gwine to hurt you," said Miss
Becky, somewhat sharply. "In my day an' time it
wuz allers took to be a bad sign when niggers got to
honeyin' 'roun' an' gwine on."

"Yessum," said Free Joe, cheerfully assenting to
the proposition — "yessum, dat's so, but me an' my
ole 'oman, we 'uz raise tergeer, en dey aint bin many
days w'en we 'uz 'way fum one 'n'er like we is now."

"Maybe she's up an' took up wi' some un else,"
said Micajah Staley from the corner. "You know
what the sayin' is, 'New master, new nigger.'"

"Dat's so, dat's de sayin', but tain't wid my ole
'oman like 'tis wid yuther niggers. Me en her wuz

des natally raise up tergeer. Dey's lots likelier
niggers dan w'at I is," said Free Joe, viewing his
shabbiness with a critical eye, "but I knows Lucindy
mos' good ez I does little Dan dar — dat I does."

There was no reply to this, and Free Joe continued, —

"Miss Becky, I wish you please, ma'am, take en
run yo' kyards en see sump'n n'er 'bout Lucindy;
kaze ef she sick, I'm gwine dar. Dey ken take en
take me up en gimme a stroppin', but I'm gwine
dar."

Miss Becky got her cards, but first she picked up
a cup, in the bottom of which were some coffee-
grounds. These she whirled slowly round and
round, ending finally by turning the cup upside down
on the hearth and allowing it to remain in that
position.

"I'll turn the cup first," said Miss Becky, "and
then I'll run the cards and see what they say."

As she shuffled the cards the fire on the hearth
burned low, and in its fitful light the gray-haired,
thin-featured woman seemed to deserve the weird
reputation which rumor and gossip had given her.
She shuffled the cards for some moments, gazing
intently in the dying fire ; then, throwing a piece of
pine on the coals, she made three divisions of the
pack, disposing them about in her lap. Then she
took the first pile, ran the cards slowly through her
fingers, and studied them carefully. To the first she

added the second pile. The study of these was
evidently not satisfactory. She said nothing, but
frowned heavily ; and the frown deepened as she
added the rest of the cards until the entire fifty-two
had passed in review before her. Though she
frowned, she seemed to be deeply interested. Without changing the relative position of the cards, she
ran them all over again. Then she threw a larger
piece of pine on the fire, shuffled the cards afresh,
divided them into three piles, and subjected them to
the same careful and critical examination.

"I can't tell the day when I've seed the cards run
this a-way," she said after a while. "What is an'
what aint, I'll never tell you ; but I know what the
cards sez."

"W'at does dey say, Miss Becky ?" the negro inquired, in a tone the solemnity of which was heightened by its eagerness.

"They er runnin' quare. These here that I'm
a-lookin' at," said Miss Becky, "they stan' for the
past. Them there, they er the present ; and the
t'others, they er the future. Here's a bundle," —
tapping the ace of clubs with her thumb, — "an'
here's a journey as plain as the nose on a man's face.
Here's Lucinda " —

"Whar she, Miss Becky ? "

" Here she is — the queen of spades."

Free Joe grinned. The idea seemed to please him
immensely.

"Well, well, well!" he exclaimed. "Ef dat don't beat my time! De queen er spades! W'en Lucindy year dat hit'll tickle 'er, sho'!"

Miss Becky continued to run the cards back and forth through her fingers.

"Here's a bundle an' a journey, and here's Lucinda. An' here's ole Spite Calderwood."

She held the cards toward the negro and touched the king of clubs.

"De Lord he'p my soul!" exclaimed Free Joe with a chuckle. "De faver's dar. Yesser, dat's him! W'at de matter 'long wid all un um, Miss Becky?"

The old woman added the second pile of cards to the first, and then the third, still running them through her fingers slowly and critically. By this time the piece of pine in the fireplace had wrapped itself in a mantle of flame, illuminating the cabin and throwing into strange relief the figure of Miss Becky as she sat studying the cards. She frowned ominously at the cards and mumbled a few words to herself. Then she dropped her hands in her lap and gazed once more into the fire. Her shadow danced and capered on the wall and floor behind her, as if, looking over her shoulder into the future, it could behold a rare spectacle. After a while she picked up the cup that had been turned on the hearth. The coffee-grounds, shaken around, presented what seemed to be a most intricate map.

"Here's the journey," said Miss Becky, presently; "here's the big road, here's rivers to cross, here's the bundle to tote." She paused and sighed. "They haint no names writ here, an' what it all means I'll never tell you. Cajy, I wish you'd be so good as to han' me my pipe."

"I haint no hand wi' the kyards," said Cajy, as he handed the pipe, "but I reckon I can patch out your misinformation, Becky, bekaze the other day, whiles I was a-finishin' up Mizzers Perdue's rollin'-pin, I hearn a rattlin' in the road. I looked out, an' Spite Calderwood was a-drivin' by in his buggy, an' thar sot Lucinda by him. It'd in-about drapt out er my min'."

Free Joe sat on the door-sill and fumbled at his hat, flinging it from one hand to the other.

"You aint see um gwine back, is you, Mars Cajy?" he asked after a while.

"Ef they went back by this road," said Mr. Staley, with the air of one who is accustomed to weigh well his words, "it must 'a' bin endurin' of the time whiles I was asleep, bekaze I haint bin no furder from my shop than to yon bed."

"Well, sir!" exclaimed Free Joe in an awed tone, which Mr. Staley seemed to regard as a tribute to his extraordinary powers of statement.

"Ef it's my beliefs you want," continued the old man, "I'll pitch 'em at you fair and free. My beliefs is that Spite Calderwood is gone an' took Lucindy

outen the county. Bless your heart and soul! when
Spite Calderwood meets the Old Boy in the road
they'll be a turrible scuffle. You mark what I tell
you."

Free Joe, still fumbling with his hat, rose and
leaned against the door-facing. He seemed to be
embarrassed. Presently he said, —

"I speck I better be gittin' 'long. Nex' time
I see Lucindy, I'm gwine tell 'er w'at Miss Becky
say 'bout de queen er spades — dat I is. Ef dat
don't tickle 'er, dey ain't no nigger 'oman never
bin tickle'."

He paused a moment, as though waiting for some
remark or comment, some confirmation of misfortune,
or, at the very least, some indorsement of his suggestion that Lucinda would be greatly pleased to know
that she had figured as the queen of spades; but
neither Miss Becky nor her brother said any thing.

"One minnit ridin' in the buggy 'longside er Mars
Spite, en de nex' highfalutin' 'roun' playin' de queen
er spades. Mon, deze yer nigger gals gittin' up in
de pictur's; dey sholy is."

With a brief "Good-night, Miss Becky, Mars
Cajy," Free Joe went out into the darkness, followed by little Dan. He made his way to the poplar, where Lucinda had been in the habit of meeting
him, and sat down. He sat there a long time; he
sat there until little Dan, growing restless, trotted
off in the direction of the Calderwood place. Dozing

against the poplar, in the gray dawn of the morning,
Free Joe heard Spite Calderwood's fox-hounds in
full cry a mile away.

"Shoo!" he exclaimed, scratching his head, and
laughing to himself, "dem ar dogs is des a-warmin'
dat old fox up."

But it was Dan the hounds were after, and the
little dog came back no more. Free Joe waited and
waited, until he grew tired of waiting. He went
back the next night and waited, and for many nights
thereafter. His waiting was in vain, and yet he
never regarded it as in vain. Careless and shabby
as he was, Free Joe was thoughtful enough to have
his theory. He was convinced that little Dan had
found Lucinda, and that some night when the moon
was shining brightly through the trees, the dog
would rouse him from his dreams as he sat sleeping
at the foot of the poplar-tree, and he would open his
eyes and behold Lucinda standing over him, laughing merrily as of old; and then he thought what fun
they would have about the queen of spades.

How many long nights Free Joe waited at the
foot of the poplar-tree for Lucinda and little Dan,
no one can ever know. He kept no account of
them, and they were not recorded by Micajah Staley
nor by Miss Becky. The season ran into summer
and then into fall. One night he went to the Staley
cabin, cut the two old people an armful of wood,
and seated himself on the door-steps, where he

rested. He was always thankful — and proud, as it
seemed — when Miss Becky gave him a cup of coffee,
which she was sometimes thoughtful enough to do.
He was especially thankful on this particular night.

"You er still layin' off for to strike up wi' Lucindy
out thar in the woods, I reckon," said Micajah
Staley, smiling grimly. The situation was not without its humorous aspects.

"Oh, dey er comin', Mars Cajy, dey er comin',
sho," Free Joe replied. "I boun' you dey'll come;
en w'en dey does come, I'll des take en fetch um
yer, whar you kin see um wid you own eyes, you en
Miss Becky."

"No," said Mr. Staley, with a quick and emphatic
gesture of disapproval. "Don't! don't fetch 'em
anywheres. Stay right wi' 'em as long as may be."

Free Joe chuckled, and slipped away into the
night, while the two old people sat gazing in the
fire. Finally Micajah spoke.

"Look at that nigger; look at 'im. He's pine-
blank as happy now as a killdee by a mill-race. You
can't 'faze 'em. I'd in-about give up my t'other
hand ef I could stan' flat-footed, an' grin at trouble
like that there nigger."

"Niggers is niggers," said Miss Becky, smiling
grimly, "an' you can't rub it out; yit I lay I've seed
a heap of white people lots meaner'n Free Joe. He
grins, — an' that's nigger, — but I've ketched his
under jaw a-trimblin' when Lucindy's name uz brung

up. An' I tell you," she went on, bridling up a little, and speaking with almost fierce emphasis, "the Old Boy's done sharpened his claws for Spite Calderwood. You'll see it."

"Me, Rebecca?" said Mr. Staley, hugging his palsied arm ; "me? I hope not."

"Well, you'll know it then," said Miss Becky, laughing heartily at her brother's look of alarm.

The next morning Micajah Staley had occasion to go into the woods after a piece of timber. He saw Free Joe sitting at the foot of the poplar, and the sight vexed him somewhat.

"Git up from there," he cried, "an' go an' arn your livin'. A mighty purty pass it's come to, when great big buck niggers can lie a-snorin' in the woods all day, when t'other folks is got to be up an' a-gwine. Git up from there!"

Receiving no response, Mr. Staley went to Free Joe, and shook him by the shoulder ; but the negro made no response. He was dead. His hat was off, his head was bent, and a smile was on his face. It was as if he had bowed and smiled when death stood before him, humble to the last. His clothes were ragged ; his hands were rough and callous ; his shoes were literally tied together with strings ; he was shabby in the extreme. A passer-by, glancing at him, could have no idea that such a humble creature had been summoned as a witness before the Lord God of Hosts.

LITTLE COMPTON.

VERY few Southern country towns have been more profitably influenced by the new order of things than Hillsborough in Middle Georgia. At various intervals since the war it has had what the local weekly calls "a business boom." The old tavern has been torn down, and in its place stands a new three-story brick hotel, managed by a very brisk young man, who is shrewd enough to advertise in the newspapers of the neighboring towns that he has "special accommodations and special rates for commercial travellers." Although Hillsborough is comparatively a small town, it is the centre of a very productive region, and its trade is somewhat important. Consequently, the commercial travellers, with characteristic energy, lose no opportunity of taking advantage of the hospitable invitation of the landlord of the Hillsborough hotel.

Not many years ago a representative of this class visited the old town. He was from the North, and, being much interested in what he saw, was duly inquisitive. Among other things that attracted his attention was a little one-armed man who seemed to be the life of the place. He was here, there, and everywhere; and wherever he went the atmosphere seemed to lighten and brighten. Sometimes he was flying around town in a buggy; at such times he was driven by a sweet-faced lady, whose smiling air of proprietorship proclaimed her to be his wife : but more often he was on foot. His cheerfulness and good humor were infectious. The old men sitting at Perdue's Corner, where they had been gathering for forty years and more, looked up and laughed as he passed ; the ladies shopping in the streets paused to chat with him ; and even the dry-goods clerks and lawyers, playing chess or draughts under the China-trees that shaded the sidewalks, were willing to be interrupted long enough to exchange jokes with him.

"Rather a lively chap that," said the observant commercial traveller.

"Well, I reckon you won't find no livelier in these diggin's," replied the landlord, to whom the remark was addressed. There was a suggestion of suppressed local pride in his tones. "He's a little chunk of a man, but he's monst'us peart."

"A colonel, I guess," said the stranger, smiling.

"Oh, no," the other rejoined. "He ain't no colonel, but he'd 'a' made a prime one. It's mighty curious to me," he went on, "that them Yankees up there didn't make him one."

"The Yankees?" inquired the commercial traveller.

"Why, yes," said the landlord. "He's a Yankee;

and that lady you seen drivin' him around, she's a
Yankee. He courted her here and he married her
here. Major Jimmy Bass wanted him to marry
her in his house, but Capt. Jack Walthall put his foot
down and said the weddin' had to be in *his* house;
d there's where it was, in that big white house
over yander with the hip roof. Yes, sir."

"Oh," said the commercial traveller, with a cyni-
cal smile, "he staid down here to keep out of the
army. He was a lucky fellow."

"Well, I reckon he was lucky not to get killed,"
said the landlord, laughing. "He fought with the
Yankees, and they do say that Little Compton was
a rattler."

The commercial traveller gave a long, low whistle,
expressive of his profound astonishment. And yet,
under all the circumstances, there was nothing to
create astonishment. The lively little man had a
history.

Among the genial and popular citizens of Hillsborough, in the days before the war, none were
more genial or more popular than Little Compton.
He was popular with all classes, with old and
with young, with whites and with blacks. He was
sober, discreet, sympathetic, and generous. He was
neither handsome nor magnetic. He was awkward
and somewhat bashful, but his manners and his conversation had the rare merit of spontaneity. His
sallow face was unrelieved by either mustache or

whiskers, and his eyes were black and very small, but they glistened with good-humor and sociabilit, He was somewhat small in stature, and for that reason the young men about Hillsborough had given him the name of Little Compton.

Little Compton's introduction to Hillsborough w? not wholly without suggestive incidents. He made his appearance there in 1850, and opened a small grocery store. Thereupon the young men of the town, with nothing better to do than to seek such amusement as they could find in so small a community, promptly proceeded to make him the victim of their pranks and practical jokes. Little Compton's forbearance was wonderful. He laughed heartily when he found his modest signboard hanging over an adjacent bar-room, and smiled good-humoredly when he found the sidewalk in front of his door barricaded with barrels and dry-goods boxes. An impatient man would have looked on these things as in the nature of indignities, but Little Compton was not an impatient man.

This went on at odd intervals, until at last the fun-loving young men began to appreciate Little Compton's admirable temper; and then for a season they played their jokes on other citizens, leaving Little Compton entirely unmolested. These young men were boisterous, but good-natured, and they had their own ideas of what constituted fair play. They were ready to fight or to have fun, but in neither case would they willingly take what they considered a mean advantage of a man.

By degrees they warmed to Little Compton. His gentleness won upon them; his patient good-humor attracted them. Without taking account of the matter, the most of them became his friends. This was demonstrated one day when one of the Pulliam boys, from Jasper County, made some slurring remark about "the little Yankee." As Pulliam was somewhat in his cups, no attention was paid to his remark; whereupon he followed it up with others of a more seriously abusive character. Little Compton was waiting on a customer; but Pulliam was standing in front of his door, and he could not fail to hear the abuse. Young Jack Walthall was sitting in a chair near the door, whittling a piece of white pine. He put his knife in his pocket, and, whistling softly, looked at Little Compton curiously. Then he walked to where Pulliam was standing.

"If I were you, Pulliam," he said, "and wanted to abuse anybody, I'd pick out a bigger man than that."

"I don't see anybody," said Pulliam.

"Well, d—— you!" exclaimed Walthall, "if you are that blind, I'll open your eyes for you!"

Whereupon he knocked Pulliam down. At this Little Compton ran out excitedly, and it was the impression of the spectators that he intended to attack the man who had been abusing him; but, instead of that, he knelt over the prostrate bully, wiped the blood from his eyes, and finally succeeded in getting him to his feet. Then Little Compton assisted him into the store, placed him in a chair, and proceeded to bandage his wounded eye. Walthall, looking on with an air of supreme indifference, uttered an exclamation of astonishment, and sauntered carelessly away.

Sauntering back an hour or so afterward, he found that Pulliam was still in Little Compton's store. He would have passed on, but Little Compton called to him. He went in prepared to be attacked, for he knew Pulliam to be one of the most dangerous men in that region, and the most revengeful; but, instead of making an attack, Pulliam offered his hand.

" Let's call it square, Jack. Your mother and my father are blood cousins, and I don't want any bad feelings to grow out of this racket. I've apologized to Mr. Compton here, and now I'm ready to apologize to you."

Walthall looked at Pulliam and at his proffered hand, and then looked at Little Compton. The latter was smiling pleasantly. This appeared to be satisfactory, and Walthall seized his kinsman's hand, and exclaimed, —

"Well, by George, Miles Pulliam! if you've apologized to Little Compton, then it's my turn to apologize to you. Maybe I was too quick with my hands, but that chap there is such a d—— clever little rascal, that it works me up to see anybody pester him."

"Why, Jack," said Compton, his little eyes glistening, "I'm not such a scrap as you make out. It's just your temper, Jack. Your temper runs clean away with your judgment."

"My temper! Why, good Lord, man! don't I just sit right down, and let folks run over me whenever they want to? Would I have done any thing if Miles Pulliam had abused *me?*"

"Why, the gilded Queen of Sheba!" exclaimed Miles Pulliam, laughing loudly, in spite of his bruises; "only last sale-day you mighty nigh jolted the life out of Bill-Tom Saunders, with the big end of a hickory stick."

"That's so," said Walthall reflectively; "but did I follow him up to do it? Wasn't he dogging after me all day, and strutting around bragging about what he was going to do? Didn't I play the little stray lamb till he rubbed his fist in my face?"

The others laughed. They knew that Jack Walthall wasn't at all lamblike in his disposition. He was tall and strong and handsome, with pale classic features, jet-black curling hair, and beautiful white hands that never knew what labor was. He was something of a dandy in Hillsborough, but in a large, manly, generous way. With his perfect manners, stately and stiff, or genial and engaging, as occasion might demand, Mr. Walthall was just such a romantic figure as one reads about in books, or as one expects to see step from behind the wings of the stage with a guitar or a long dagger. Indeed, he was the veritable original of Cyrille Brandon, the hero of Miss Amelia Baxter's elegant novel entitled " The Haunted Manor ; or, Souvenirs of the Sunny Southland." If those who are fortunate enough to possess a copy of this graphic book, which was printed in Charleston for the author, will turn to the description of Cyrille Brandon, they will get a much better idea of Mr. Walthall than they can hope to get in this brief and imperfect chronicle. It is true, the picture there drawn is somewhat exaggerated to suit the purposes of fictive art, but it shows perfectly the serious impression Mr. Walthall made on the ladies who were his contemporaries.

It is only fair to say, however, that the real Mr. Walthall was altogether different from the ideal Cyrille Brandon of Miss Baxter's powerfully written book. He was by no means ignorant of the impression he made on the fair sex, and he was somewhat proud of it ; but he had no romantic ideas of his own. He was, in fact, a very practical young man. When the Walthall estate, composed of thousands of acres of land and several hundred healthy, well-fed negroes, was divided up, he chose to take his portion in money ; and this he loaned out at a fair interest to those who were in need of ready cash. This gave him large leisure ; and, as was the custom among the young men of leisure, he gambled a little when the humor was on him, having the judgment and the nerve to make the game of poker exceedingly interesting to those who sat with him at table.

No one could ever explain why the handsome and gallant Jack Walthall should go so far as to stand between his own cousin and Little Compton; indeed, no one tried to explain it. The fact was accepted for what it was worth, and it was a great deal to Little Compton in a social and business way. After the row which has just been described, Mr. Walthall was usually to be found at Compton's store, — in the summer sitting in front of the door under the grateful shade of the China-trees, and in the winter sitting by the comfortable fire that Compton kept burning in his back room. As Mr. Walthall was the recognized leader of the young men, Little Compton's store soon became the headquarters for all of them. They met there, and they made themselves at home there, introducing their affable host to many queer antics and capers peculiar to the youth of that day and time, and to the social organism of which that youth was the outcome.

That Little Compton enjoyed their company, is certain; but it is doubtful if he entered heartily into the plans of their escapades, which they freely discussed around his hearth. Perhaps it was because he had outlived the folly of youth. Though his face was smooth and round, and his eye bright,

Little Compton bore the marks of maturity and experience. He used to laugh, and say that he was
born in New Jersey, and died there when he was
young. What significance this statement possessed,
no one ever knew ; probably no one in Hillsborough
cared to know. The people of that town had their
own notions and their own opinions. They were not
unduly inquisitive, save when their inquisitiveness
seemed to take a political shape ; and then it was
somewhat aggressive.

There were a great many things in Hillsborough
likely to puzzle a stranger. Little Compton observed
that the young men, no matter how young they
might be, were absorbed in politics. They had the
political history of the country at their tongues'
ends, and the discussions they carried on were inter-
minable. This interest extended to all classes : the
planters discussed politics with their overseers ; and
lawyers, merchants, tradesmen, and gentlemen of
elegant leisure, discussed politics with each other.
Schoolboys knew all about the Missouri Compro-
mise, the fugitive-slave law, and States rights. Sometimes the arguments used were more substantial than
mere words, but this was only when some old feud
was back of the discussion. There was one question, as Little Compton discovered, in regard to
which there was no discussion. That question was
slavery. It loomed up everywhere and in every
thing, and was the basis of all the arguments, and

yet it was not discussed : there was no room for discussion. There was but one idea, and that was that slavery must be defended at all hazards, and against all enemies. That was the temper of the time, and Little Compton was not long in discovering that of all dangerous issues slavery was the most dangerous.

The young men, in their free-and-easy way, told him the story of a wayfarer who once came through that region preaching abolitionism to the negroes. The negroes themselves betrayed him, and he was promptly taken in charge. His body was found afterward hanging in the woods, and he was buried at the expense of the county. Even his name had been forgotten, and his grave was all but obliterated. All these things made an impression on Little Compton's mind. The tragedy itself was recalled by one of the pranks of the young men, that was conceived and carried out under his eyes. It happened after he had become well used to the ways of Hillsborough. There came a stranger to the town, whose queer acts excited the suspicions of a naturally suspicious community. Professedly he was a colporteur ; but, instead of trying to dispose of books and tracts, of which he had a visible supply, he devoted himself to arguing with the village politicians under the shade of the trees. It was observed, also, that he would frequently note down observations in a memorandum-book. Just about that time the con-

troversy between the slaveholders and the abolitionists was at its height. John Brown had made his
raid on Harper's Ferry, and there was a good deal of
excitement throughout the South. It was rumored
that Brown had emissaries travelling from State to
State, preparing the negroes for insurrection ; and
every community, even Hillsborough, was on the
alert, watching, waiting, suspecting.

The time assuredly was not auspicious for the
stranger with the ready memorandum-book. Sitting
in front of Compton's store, he fell into conversation
one day with Uncle Abner Lazenberry, a patriarch
who lived in the country, and who had a habit of
coming to Hillsborough at least once a week to "talk
with the boys." Uncle Abner belonged to the poorer
class of planters ; that is to say, he had a small farm
and not more than half a dozen negroes. But he
was decidedly popular, and his conversation — somewhat caustic at times — was thoroughly enjoyed by
the younger generation. On this occasion he had
been talking to Jack Walthall, when the stranger
drew a chair within hearing distance.

"You take all your men," Uncle Abner was saying — "take all un 'em, but gimme Hennery Clay.
Them abolishioners, they may come an' git all six er
my niggers, if they'll jess but lemme keep the ginny-
wine ole Whig docterin'. Thát's me up an' down —
that's wher' your Uncle Abner Lazenberry stan's,
boys." By this time the stranger had taken out his

inevitable note-book, and Uncle Abner went on: "Yes, siree! You may jess mark me down that away. 'Come,' sez I, 'an' take all my niggers an' the ole gray mar',' sez I, 'but lemme keep my Whig docterin',' sez I. Lord, I've seed sights wi' them niggers. They hain't no manner account. They won't work, an' I'm ablidge to feed 'em, else they'd whirl in an' steal from the neighbors. Hit's in-about broke me for to maintain 'em in the'r laziness. Bless your soul, little childern! I'm in a turrible fix — a turrible fix. I'm that bankruptured that when I come to town, ef I fine a thrip in my britches-pocket for to buy me a dram I'm the happiest mortal in the county. Yes, siree! hit's got down to that."

Here Uncle Abner Lazenberry paused and eyed the stranger shrewdly, to whom, presently, he addressed himself in a very insinuating tone : —

"What mought be your name, mister ?"

"Oh," said the stranger, taken somewhat aback by the suddenness of the question, "my name might be Jones, but it happens to be Davies."

Uncle Abner Lazenberry stared at Davies a moment as if amazed, and then exclaimed, —

"Jesso! Well, dog my cats ef times hain't a-changin' an' a-changin' tell bimeby the natchul world an' all the hummysp'eres 'll make the'r disappearance een'-uppermost. Yit, whiles they er changin' an' a-disappearin', I hope they'll leave me my ole Whig docterin', an' my name, which the fust

an' last un it is Abner Lazenberry. An' more'n
that," the old man went on, with severe emphasis, —
"an' more'n that, they hain't never been a day sence
the creation of the world an' the hummysp'eres when
my name mought er been any thing else under the
shinin' sun but Abner Lazenberry ; an' ef the time's
done come when any mortal name mought er been
any thing but what hit reely is, then we jess better
turn the nation an' the federation over to demock-
eracy an' giner'l damnation. Now that's me, right
pine-plank."

By way of emphasizing his remarks, Uncle Abner
brought the end of his hickory cane down upon the
ground with a tremendous thump. The stranger
reddened a little at the unexpected criticism, and was
evidently ill at ease, but he remarked politely, —

"This is just a saying I've picked up somewhere
in my travels. My name is Davies, and I am travel-
ing through the country selling a few choice books,
and picking up information as I go."

"I know a mighty heap of Davises," said Uncle
Abner, "but I disremember of anybody name
Davies."

"Well, sir," said Mr. Davies, "the name is not
uncommon in my part of the country. I am from
Vermont."

"Well, well!" said Uncle Abner, tapping the
ground thoughtfully with his cane. "A mighty fur
ways Vermont is, tooby shore. In my day an' time

I've seed as many as three men folks from Vermont,
an' one un 'em, he wuz a wheelwright, an' one wuz
a tin-peddler, an' the yuther one wuz a clock-maker.
But that wuz a long time ago. How is the abolishioners gittin' on up that away, an' when in the name
er patience is they a-comin' arter my niggers? Lord!
if them niggers wuz free, I wouldn't have to slave for
'em."

"Well, sir," said Mr. Davies, "I take little or no
interest in those things. I have to make a humble
living, and I leave political questions to the politicians."

The conversation was carried on at some length,
the younger men joining in occasionally to ask questions; and nothing could have been friendlier than
their attitude toward Mr. Davies. They treated him
with the greatest consideration. His manner and
speech were those of an educated man, and he
seemed to make himself thoroughly agreeable. But
that night, as Mr. Jack Walthall was about to go to
bed, his body-servant, a negro named Jake, began
to question him about the abolitionists.

"What do you know about abolitionists?" Mr.
Walthall asked with some degree of severity.

"Nothin' 'tall, Marse Jack, 'cep'in' w'at dish yer
new w'ite man down dar at de tavern say."

"And what did he say?" Mr. Walthall inquired.

"I ax 'im, I say, 'Marse Boss, is dese yer bobolitionists got horns en huffs?' en he 'low, he did, dat

dey ain't no bobolitionists, kaze dey er babolitionists,
an' dey ain't got needer horns ner huffs."

"What else did he say?"

Jake laughed. It was a hearty and humorous
laugh.

"Well, sir," he replied, "dat man des preached.
He sholy did. He ax me ef de niggers 'roun' yer
wouldn' all like ter be free, en I tole 'im I don't speck
dey would, kase all de free niggers w'at I ever seed
is de mos' no-'countes' niggers in de lan'."

Mr. Walthall dismissed the negro somewhat curtly.
He had prepared to retire for the night, but apparently thought better of it, for he resumed his coat
and vest, and went out into the cool moonlight. He
walked around the public square, and finally perched
himself on the stile that led over the court-house
enclosure. He sat there a long time. Little Compton passed by, escorting Miss Lizzie Fairleigh, the
schoolmistress, home from some social gathering;
and finally the lights in the village went out one by
one — all save the one that shone in the window of
the room occupied by Mr. Davies. Watching this
window somewhat closely, Mr. Jack Walthall observed that there was movement in the room. Shadows played on the white window-curtains — human
shadows passing to and fro. The curtains, quivering
in the night wind, distorted these shadows, and made
confusion of them; but the wind died away for a
moment, and, outlined on the curtains, the patient

watcher saw a silhouette of Jake, his body-servant. Mr. Walthall beheld the spectacle with amazement. It never occurred to him that the picture he saw was part — the beginning indeed — of a tremendous panorama which would shortly engage the attention of the civilized world, but he gazed at it with a feeling of vague uneasiness.

The next morning Little Compton was somewhat surprised at the absence of the young men who were in the habit of gathering in front of his store. Even Mr. Jack Walthall, who could be depended on to tilt his chair against the China-tree and sit there for an hour or more after breakfast, failed to put in an appearance. After putting his store to rights, and posting up some accounts left over from the day before, Little Compton came out on the sidewalk, and walked up and down in front of the door. He was in excellent humor, and as he walked he hummed a tune. He did not lack for companionship, for his cat, Tommy Tinktums, an extraordinarily large one, followed him back and forth, rubbing against him and running between his legs ; but somehow he felt lonely. The town was very quiet. It was quiet at all times, but on this particular morning it seemed to Little Compton that there was less stir than usual. There was no sign of life anywhere around the public square save at Perdue's Corner. Shading his eyes with his hand, Little Compton observed a group of citizens apparently engaged in a very interesting discussion. Among them he recognized the tall form of Mr. Jack Walthall and the somewhat ponderous presence of Major Jimmy Bass. Little Compton watched the group because he had nothing better to do. He saw Major Jimmy Bass bring the end of his cane down upon the ground with a tremendous thump, and gesticulate like a man laboring under strong excitement ; but this was nothing out of the ordinary, for Major Jimmy had been known to get excited over the most trivial discussion ; on one occasion, indeed, he had even mounted a dry-goods box, and, as the boys expressed it, " cussed out the town."

Still watching the group, Little Compton saw Mr. Jack Walthall take Buck Ransome by the arm, and walk across the public square in the direction of the court-house. They were followed by Mr. Alvin Cozart, Major Jimmy Bass, and young Rowan Wornum. They went to the court-house stile, and formed a little group, while Mr. Walthall appeared to be explaining something, pointing frequently in the direction of the tavern. In a little while they returned to those they had left at Perdue's Corner, where they were presently joined by a number of other citizens. Once Little Compton thought he would lock his door and join them, but by the time he had made up his mind the group had dispersed.

A little later on, Compton's curiosity was more than satisfied. One of the young men, Buck Ransome, came into Compton's store, bringing a queer-

looking bundle. Unwrapping it, Mr. Ransome
brought to view two large pillows. Whistling a gay
tune, he ran his keen knife into one of these, and felt
of the feathers. His manner was that of an expert.
The examination seemed to satisfy him ; for he rolled
the pillows into a bundle again, and deposited them
in the back part of the store.

"You'd be a nice housekeeper, Buck, if you did all
your pillows that way," said Compton.

"Why, bless your great big soul, Compy," said
Mr. Ransome, striking an attitude, "I'm the finest in
the land."

Just then Mr. Alvin Cozart came in, bearing a
small bucket, which he handled very carefully. Little
Compton thought he detected the odor of tar.

"Stick her in the back room there," said Mr.
Ransome ; "she'll keep."

Compton was somewhat mystified by these proceedings ; but every thing was made clear when, an
hour later, the young men of the town, re-enforced
by Major Jimmy Bass, marched into his store, bringing with them Mr. Davies, the Vermont colporteur,
who had been flourishing his note-book in the faces
of the inhabitants. Jake, Mr. Walthall's body-servant, was prominent in the crowd by reason of his
color and his frightened appearance. The colporteur was very pale, but he seemed to be cool. As
the last one filed in, Mr. Walthall stepped to the
front door and shut and locked it. Compton was

too amazed to say any thing. The faces before him, always so full of humor and fun, were serious enough now. As the key turned in the lock, the colporteur found his voice.

"Gentlemen!" he exclaimed with some show of indignation, "what is the meaning of this? What would you do?"

"You know mighty well, sir, what we ought to do," cried Major Bass. "We ought to hang you, you imperdent scounderl! A-comin' down here a-pesterin' an' a-meddlin' with t'other people's business."

"Why, gentlemen," said Davies, "I'm a peaceable citizen; I trouble nobody. I am simply travelling through the country selling books to those who are able to buy, and giving them away to those who are not."

"Mr. Davies," said Mr. Jack Walthall, leaning gracefully against the counter, "what kind of books are you selling?"

"Religious books, sir."

"Jake!" exclaimed Mr. Walthall somewhat sharply, so sharply, indeed, that the negro jumped as though he had been shot. "Jake! stand out there. Hold up your head, sir! — Mr. Davies, how many religious books did you sell to that nigger there last night?"

"I sold him none, sir; I" —

"How many did you *try* to sell him?"

"I made no attempt to sell him any books; I

knew he couldn't read. I merely asked him to give
me some information."

Major Jimmy Bass scowled dreadfully; but Mr.
Jack Walthall smiled pleasantly, and turned to the
negro.

"Jake! do you know this man?"

"I seed 'im, Marse Jack; I des seed 'im; dat's all
I know 'bout 'im."

"What were you doing sasshaying around in his
room last night?"

Jake scratched his head, dropped his eyes, and
shuffled about on the floor with his feet. All eyes
were turned on him. He made so long a pause that
Alvin Cozart remarked in his drawling tone, —

"Jack, hadn't we better take this nigger over to
the calaboose?"

"Not yet," said Mr. Walthall pleasantly. "If I
have to take him over there I'll not bring him back
in a hurry."

"I wuz des up in his room kaze he tole me fer ter
come back en see 'im. Name er God, Marse Jack,
w'at ail' you all w'ite folks now?"

"What did he say to you?" asked Mr. Walthall.

"He ax me w'at make de niggers stay in slave'y,"
said the frightened negro; "he ax me w'at de reason
dey don't git free deyse'f."

"He was warm after information," Mr. Walthall
suggested.

"Call it what you please," said the Vermont col-

porteur. " I asked him those questions and more."
He was pale, but he no longer acted like a man
troubled with fear.

"Oh, we know that, mister," said Buck Ransome.
" We know what you come for, and we know what
you're goin' away for. We'll excuse you if you'll
excuse us, and then there'll be no hard feelin's —
that is, not many ; none to growl about. — Jake, hand
me that bundle there on the barrel, and fetch that
tar-bucket. — You've got the makin' of a mighty fine
bird in you, mister," Ransome went on, addressing
the colporteur ; "all you lack's the feathers, and
we've got oodles of 'em right here. Now, will you
shuck them duds?"

For the first time the fact dawned on Little
Compton's mind, that the young men were about to
administer a coat of tar and feathers to the stranger
from Vermont ; and he immediately began to protest.

"Why, Jack," said he, " what has the man done?"

"Well," replied Mr. Walthall, "you heard what
the nigger said. We can't afford to have these
abolitionists preaching insurrection right in our back
yards. We just can't afford it, that's the long and
short of it. Maybe you don't understand it ; maybe
you don't feel as we do ; but that's the way the
matter stands. We are in a sort of a corner, and
we are compelled to protect ourselves."

"I don't believe in no tar and feathers for this
chap," remarked Major Jimmy Bass, assuming a

judicial air. "He'll just go out here to the town branch and wash 'em off, and then he'll go on through the plantations raising h—— among the niggers. That'll be the upshot of it — now, you mark my words. He ought to be hung."

"Now, boys," said Little Compton, still protesting, "what is the use? This man hasn't done any real harm. He might preach insurrection around here for a thousand years, and the niggers wouldn't listen to him. Now, you know that yourselves. Turn the poor devil loose, and let him get out of town. Why, haven't you got any confidence in the niggers you've raised yourselves?"

"My dear sir," said Rowan Wornum, in his most insinuating tone, "we've got all the confidence in the world in the niggers, but we can't afford to take any risks. Why, my dear sir," he went on, "if we let this chap go, it won't be six months before the whole country'll be full of this kind. Look at that Harper's Ferry business."

"Well," said Compton somewhat hotly, "look at it. What harm has been done? Has there been any nigger insurrection?"

Jack Walthall laughed good-naturedly. "Little Compton is a quick talker, boys. Let's give the man the benefit of all the arguments."

"Great God! You don't mean to let this d—— rascal go, do you, Jack?" exclaimed Major Jimmy Bass.

" No, no, sweet uncle; but I've got a nicer dose than tar and feathers."

The result was that the stranger's face and hands were given a coat of lampblack, his arms were tied to his body, and a large placard was fastened to his back. The placard bore this inscription:

> ABOLITIONIST!
> PASS HIM ON, BOYS.

Mr. Davies was a pitiful-looking object after the young men had plastered his face and hands with lampblack and oil, and yet his appearance bore a certain queer relation to the humorous exhibitions one sees on the negro minstrel stage. Particularly was this the case when he smiled at Compton.

"By George, boys!" exclaimed Mr. Buck Ransome, "this chap could play Old Bob Ridley at the circus."

When every thing was arranged to suit them, the young men formed a procession, and marched the blackened stranger from Little Compton's door into the public street. Little Compton seemed to be very much interested in the proceeding. It was remarked afterward, that he seemed to be very much agitated, and that he took a position very near the placarded abolitionist. The procession, as it moved up the street, attracted considerable attention. Rumors that an abolitionist was to be dealt with had appar-

ently been circulated, and a majority of the male inhabitants of the town were out to view the spectacle.
The procession passed entirely around the public
square, of which the court-house was the centre, and
then across the square to the park-like enclosure
that surrounded the temple of justice.

As the young men and their prisoner crossed this
open space, Major Jimmy Bass, fat as he was, grew
so hilarious that he straddled his cane as children do
broomsticks, and pretended that he had as much as
he could do to hold his fiery wooden steed. He
waddled and pranced out in front of the abolitionist,
and turned and faced him, whereat his steed showed
the most violent symptoms of running away. The
young men roared with laughter, and the spectators
roared with them, and even the abolitionist laughed.
All laughed but Little Compton. The procession
was marched to the court-house enclosure, and there
the prisoner was made to stand on the sale-block
so that all might have a fair view of him. He was
kept there until the stage was ready to go; and
then he was given a seat on that swaying vehicle,
and forwarded to Rockville, where, presumably, the
"boys" placed him on the train and "passed him
on" to the "boys" in other towns.

For months thereafter there was peace in Hillsborough, so far as the abolitionists were concerned;
and then came the secession movement. A majority
of the citizens of the little town were strong Union

men; but the secession movement seemed to take
even the oldest off their feet, and by the time the
Republican President was inaugurated, the Union
sentiment that had marked Hillsborough had practically disappeared.   In South Carolina companies of
minute-men had been formed, and the entire white
male population was wearing blue cockades.   With
some modifications, these symptoms were reproduced
in Hillsborough.   The modifications were that a few
of the old men still stood up for the Union, and that
some of the young men, though they wore the blue
cockade, did not align themselves with the minute-
men.

Little Compton took no part in these proceedings.
He was discreetly quiet.   He tended his store, and
smoked his pipe, and watched events.   One morning
he was aroused from his slumbers by a tremendous
crash, — a crash that rattled the windows of his store
and shook its very walls.   He lay quiet a while, thinking that a small earthquake had been turned loose on
the town.   Then the crash was repeated; and he
knew that Hillsborough was firing a salute from its
little six-pounder, a relic of the Revolution, that had
often served the purpose of celebrating the nation's
birthday in a noisily becoming manner.

Little Compton arose, and dressed himself, and
prepared to put his store in order.   Issuing forth into
the street, he saw that the town was in considerable
commotion.   A citizen who had been in attendance

on the convention at Milledgeville had arrived during the night, bringing the information that the ordinance of secession had been adopted, and that Georgia was now a sovereign and independent government. The original secessionists were in high feather, and their hilarious enthusiasm had its effect on all save a few of the Union men.

Early as it was, Little Compton saw two flags floating from an improvised flagstaff on top of the court-house. One was the flag of the State, with its pillars, its sentinel, and its legend of " Wisdom, Justice, and Moderation." The design of the other was entirely new to Little Compton. It was a pine-tree on a field of white, with a rattlesnake coiled at its roots, and the inscription, "DON'T TREAD ON ME!" A few hours later Uncle Abner Lazenberry made his appearance in front of Compton's store. He had just hitched his horse to the rack near the court-house.

" Merciful heavens!" he exclaimed, wiping his red face with a red handkerchief, " is the Ole Boy done gone an' turned hisself loose? I hearn the racket, an' I sez to the ole woman, sez I, ' I'll fling the saddle on the gray mar' an' canter to town an' see what in the dingnation the matter is. An' ef the worl's about to fetch a lurch, I'll git me another dram an' die happy,' sez I. Whar's Jack Walthall? He can tell his Uncle Abner all about it."

" Well, sir," said Little Compton. "the State has seceded, and the boys are celebrating."

"I know'd it," cried the old man angrily. "My min' tole me so." Then he turned and looked at the flags flying from the top of the court-house. "Is them rags the things they er gwine to fly out'n the Union with?" he exclaimed scornfully. "Why, bless your soul an' body, hit'll take bigger wings than them! Well, sir, I'm sick; I am that away. I wuz born in the Union, an' I'd like mighty well to die thar. Ain't it mine? ain't it our'n? Jess as shore as you're born, thar's trouble ahead — big trouble. You're from the North, ain't you?" Uncle Abner asked, looking curiously at Little Compton.

"Yes, sir, I am," Compton replied; "that is, I am from New Jersey, but they say New Jersey is out of the Union."

Uncle Abner did not respond to Compton's smile. He continued to gaze at him significantly.

"Well," the old man remarked somewhat bluntly, "you better go back where you come from. You ain't got nothin' in the roun' worl' to do with all this hellabaloo. When the pinch comes, as come it must, I'm jes gwine to swap a nigger for a sack er flour an' settle down; but you had better go back where you come from."

Little Compton knew the old man was friendly; but his words, so solemnly and significantly uttered, made a deep impression. The words recalled to Compton's mind the spectacle of the man from Vermont who had been paraded through the streets

of Hillsborough, with his face blackened and a placard on his back. The little Jerseyman also recalled
other incidents, some of them trifling enough, but
all of them together going to show the hot temper
of the people around him; and for a day or two he
brooded rather seriously over the situation. He
knew that the times were critical.

For several weeks the excitement in Hillsborough,
as elsewhere in the South, continued to run high.
The blood of the people was at fever heat. The air
was full of the portents and premonitions of war.
Drums were beating, flags were flying, and military
companies were parading. Jack Walthall had raised
a company, and it had gone into camp in an old field
near the town. The tents shone snowy white in the
sun, the uniforms of the men were bright and gay,
and the boys thought this was war. But, instead of
that, they were merely enjoying a holiday. The
ladies of the town sent them wagon-loads of provisions every day, and the occasion was a veritable
picnic, — a picnic that some of the young men remembered a year or two later when they were trudg-
ing ragged, barefooted, and hungry, through the
snow and slush of a Virginian winter.

But, with all their drilling and parading in the
peaceful camp at Hillsborough, the young men had
many idle hours, and they devoted these to various
forms of amusements. On one occasion, after they
had exhausted their ingenuity in search of entertain-

ment, one of them, Lieut. Buck Ransome, suggested that it might be interesting to get up a joke on Little Compton.

"But how?" asked Lieut. Cozart.

"Why, the easiest in the world," said Lieut. Ransome. "Write him a note, and tell him that the time has come for an English-speaking people to take sides, and fling in a kind of side-wiper about New Jersey."

Capt. Jack Walthall, leaning comfortably against a huge box that was supposed to bear some relation to a camp-chest, blew a cloud of smoke through his sensitive nostrils and laughed. "Why, stuff, boys!" he exclaimed somewhat impatiently, "you can't scare Little Compton. He's got grit, and it's the right kind of grit. Why, I'll tell you what's a fact, — the sand in that man's gizzard would make enough mortar to build a fort."

"Well, I'll tell you what we'll do," said Lieut. Ransome. "We'll sling him a line or two, and if it don't stir him up, all right; but if it does, we'll have some tall fun."

Whereupon, Lieut. Ransome fished around in the chest, and drew forth pen and ink and paper. With some aid from his brother officers he managed to compose the following : —

"LITTLE MR. COMPTON. *Dear Sir,* — The time has arrived when every man should show his colors. Those who are not for us are against us. Your best friends, when asked where you stand, do not know what to say. If you are for the North in this struggle, your place is at the North. If you are for the South, your place is with those who are preparing to defend the rights and liberties of the South. A word to the wise is sufficient. You will hear from me again in due time.

"NEMESIS."

This was duly sealed and dropped in the Hillsborough post-office, and Little Compton received it the same afternoon. He smiled as he broke the seal, but ceased to smile when he read the note. It happened to fit a certain vague feeling of uneasiness that possessed him. He laid it down on his desk, walked up and down behind his counter, and then returned and read it again. The sprawling words seemed to possess a fascination for him. He read them again and again, and turned them over and over in his mind. It was characteristic of his simple nature, that he never once attributed the origin of the note to the humor of the young men with whom he was so familiar. He regarded it seriously. Looking up from the note, he could see in the corner of his store the brush and pot that had been used as arguments on the Vermont abolitionist. He vividly recalled the time when that unfortunate person was brought up before the self-constituted tribunal that assembled in his store.

Little Compton thought he had gauged accurately the temper of the people about him ; and he had, but his modesty prevented him from accurately gauging,

or even thinking about, the impression he had made
on them. The note troubled him a good deal more
than he would at first confess to himself. He seated
himself on a low box behind his counter to think it
over, resting his face in his hands. A little boy who
wanted to buy a thrip's worth of candy went slowly
out again after trying in vain to attract the attention
of the hitherto prompt and friendly store-keeper.
Tommy Tinktums, the cat, seeing that his master
was sitting down, came forward with the expectation
of being told to perform his famous "bouncing"
trick, a feat that was at once the wonder and delight
of the youngsters around Hillsborough. But Tommy
Tinktums was not commanded to bounce ; and so
he contented himself with washing his face, pausing
every now and then to watch his master with half-
closed eyes.

While sitting thus reflecting, it suddenly occurred
to Little Compton that he had had very few cus-
tomers during the past several days ; and it seemed
to him, as he continued to think the matter over,
that the people, especially the young men, had been
less cordial lately than they had ever been before.
It never occurred to him that the threatened war,
and the excitement of the period, occupied their
entire attention. He simply remembered that the
young men who had made his modest little store
their headquarters met there no more. Little Compton sat behind his counter a long time thinking.

The sun went down, and the dusk fell, and the night came on and found him there.

After a while he lit a candle, spread the communication out on his desk, and read it again. To his mind, there was no mistaking its meaning. It meant that he must either fight against the Union, or array against himself all the bitter and aggressive suspicion of the period. He sighed heavily, closed his store, and went out into the darkness. He made his way to the residence of Major Jimmy Bass, where Miss Lizzie Fairleigh boarded. The major himself was sitting on the veranda; and he welcomed Little Compton with effusive hospitality, — a hospitality that possessed an old-fashioned flavor.

"I'm mighty glad you come, — yes, sir, I am. It looks like the whole world's out at the camps, and it makes me feel sorter lonesome. Yes, sir; it does that. If I wasn't so plump I'd be out there too. It's a mighty good place to be about this time of the year. I tell you what, sir, them boys is got the devil in 'em. Yes, sir; there ain't no two ways about that. When they turn themselves loose, somebody or something will git hurt. Now, you mark what I tell you. It's a tough lot, — a mighty tough lot. Lord! wouldn't I hate to be a Yankee, and fall in their hands! I'd be glad if I had time for to say my prayers. Yes, sir; I would that."

Thus spoke the cheerful Major Bass; and every word he said seemed to rhyme with Little Compton's own thoughts, and to confirm the fears that had been aroused by the note. After he had listened to the major a while, Little Compton asked for Miss Fairleigh.

"Oho!" said the major. Then he called to a negro who happened to be passing through the hall, "Jesse, tell Miss Lizzie that Mr. Compton is in the parlor." Then he turned to Compton. "I tell you what, sir, that gal looks mighty puny. She's from the North, and I reckon she's homesick. And then there's all this talk about war. She knows our boys'll eat the Yankees plum up, and I don't blame her for being sorter down-hearted. I wish you'd try to cheer her up. She's a good gal if there ever was one on the face of the earth."

Little Compton went into the parlor, where he was presently joined by Miss Fairleigh. They talked a long time together, but what they said no one ever knew. They conversed in low tones; and once or twice the hospitable major, sitting on the veranda, detected himself trying to hear what they said. He could see them from where he sat, and he observed that both appeared to be profoundly dejected. Not once did they laugh, or, so far as the major could see, even smile. Occasionally Little Compton arose and walked the length of the parlor, but Miss Fairleigh sat with bowed head. It may have been a trick of the lamp, but it seemed to the major that they were both very pale.

Finally Little Compton rose to go. The major observed with a chuckle that he held Miss Fairleigh's hand a little longer than was strictly necessary under the circumstances. He held it so long, indeed, that Miss Fairleigh half averted her face, but the major noted that she was still pale. "We shall have a wedding in this house before the war opens," he thought to himself; and his mind was dwelling on such a contingency when Little Compton came out on the veranda.

"Don't tear yourself away in the heat of the day," said Major Bass jocularly.

"I must go," replied Compton. "Good-by!" He seized the major's hand and wrung it.

"Good-night," said the major, "and God bless you!"

The next day was Sunday. But on Monday it was observed that Compton's store was closed. Nothing was said and little thought of it. People's minds were busy with other matters. The drums were beating, the flags flying, and the citizen soldiery parading. It was a noisy and an exciting time, and a larger store than Little Compton's might have remained closed for several days without attracting attention. But one day, when the young men from the camp were in the village, it occurred to them to inquire what effect the anonymous note had had on Little Compton; whereupon they went in a body to his store; but the door was closed, and they found

it had been closed a week or more. They also discovered that Compton had disappeared.

This had a very peculiar effect upon Capt. Jack
Walthall. He took off his uniform, put on his citizen's clothes, and proceeded to investigate Compton's
disappearance. He sought in vain for a clew. He
interested others to such an extent that a great
many people in Hillsborough forgot all about the
military situation. But there was no trace of Little
Compton. His store was entered from a rear window, and every thing found to be intact. Nothing
had been removed. The jars of striped candy that
had proved so attractive to the youngsters of Hillsborough stood in long rows on the shelves, flanked
by the thousand and one notions that make up the
stock of a country grocery store. Little Compton's
disappearance was a mysterious one, and under ordinary circumstances would have created intense excitement in the community ; but at that particular
time the most sensational event would have seemed
tame and commonplace alongside the preparations
for war.

Owing probably to a lack of the faculty of organi-
zation at Richmond, — a lack which, if we are to
believe the various historians who have tried to
describe and account for some of the results of that
period, was the cause of many bitter controversies,
and of many disastrous failures in the field, — a
month or more passed away before the Hillsborough

company received orders to go to the front. Fort
Sumter had been fired on, troops from all parts of
the South had gathered in Virginia, and the war was
beginning in earnest. Capt. Jack Walthall of the
Hillsborough Guards chafed at the delay that kept
his men resting on their arms, so to speak ; but he
had ample opportunity, meanwhile, to wonder what
had become of Little Compton. In his leisure
moments he often found himself sitting on the dry-
goods boxes in the neighborhood of Little Compton's
store. Sitting thus one day, he was approached by
his body-servant. Jake had his hat in his hand, and
showed by his manner that he had something to say.
He shuffled around, looked first one way and then
another, and scratched his head.

"Marse Jack," he began.

"Well, what is it?" said the other, somewhat
sharply.

"Marse Jack, I hope ter de Lord you ain't gwine
ter git mad wid me ; yit I mos' knows you is, kaze I
oughter done tole you a long time ago."

"You ought to have told me what?"

"'Bout my drivin' yo' hoss en buggy over ter
Rockville dat time, — dat time what I ain't never
tole you 'bout. But I 'uz mos' 'blige' ter do it. I
'low ter myse'f, I did, dat I oughter come tell you
right den, but I 'uz skeer'd you mought git mad, en
den you wuz out dar at de camps, 'long wid dem
milliumterry folks."

"What have you got to tell?"

"Well, Marse Jack, des 'bout takin' yo' hoss en buggy. Marse Compton 'lowed you wouldn't keer, en w'en he say dat, I des went en hitch up de hoss en kyar'd 'im over ter Rockville."

"What under heaven did you want to go to Rockville for?"

"Who? me, Marse Jack? 'Twa'n't me wanter go. Hit 'uz Marse Compton."

"Little Compton?" exclaimed Walthall.

"Yes, sir, dat ve'y same man."

"What did you carry Little Compton to Rockville for?"

"Fo' de Lord, Marse Jack, I dunno w'at Marse Compton wanter go fer. I des know'd I 'uz doin' wrong, but he tuck'n 'low' dat hit'd be all right wid you, kaze you bin knowin' him so monst'us well. En den he up'n ax me not to tell you twell he done plum out'n yearin'."

"Didn't he say any thing? Didn't he tell you where he was going? Didn't he send any word back?"

This seemed to remind Jake of something. He clapped his hand to his head, and exclaimed, —

"Well, de Lord he'p my soul! Ef I ain't de beatenest nigger on de top side er de yeth! Marse Compton gun me a letter, en I tuck'n shove it un' de buggy seat, en it's right dar yit ef somebody ain't tored it up."

By certain well-known signs Jake knew that his
· Marse Jack was very mad, and he was hurrying out.
But Walthall called him.

"Come here, sir!" The tone made Jake tremble.
"Do you stand up there, sir, and tell me all this, and
think I am going to put up with it?"

"I'm gwine after dat note, Marse Jack, des ez
hard ez ever I kin."

Jake managed to find the note after some little
search, and carried it to Jack Walthall. It was
crumpled and soiled. It had evidently seen rough
service under the buggy seat. Walthall took it from
the negro, turned it over and looked at it. It was
sealed, and addressed to Miss Lizzie Fairleigh.

Jack Walthall arrayed himself in his best, and
made his way to Major Jimmy Bass's, where he
inquired for Miss Fairleigh. That young lady
promptly made her appearance. She was pale and
seemed to be troubled. Walthall explained his
errand, and handed her the note. He thought her
hand trembled, but he may have been mistaken, as
he afterward confessed. She read it, and handed it
to Capt. Walthall with a vague little smile that
would have told him volumes if he had been able to
read the feminine mind.

Major Jimmy Bass was a wiser man than Walthall,
and he remarked long afterward that he knew by the
way the poor girl looked that she was in trouble, and
it is not to be denied, at least, it is not to be denied

in Hillsborough, where he was known and respected
— that Major Bass's impressions were as important
as the average man's convictions. This is what
Capt. Jack Walthall read : —

"DEAR MISS FAIRLEIGH, — When you see this I shall be
on my way home. My eyes have recently been opened to the
fact that there is to be a war for and against the Union. I have
strong friendships here, but I feel that I owe a duty to the old
flag. When I bade you good-by last night, it was good-by forever. I had hoped — I had desired — to say more than I did ;
but perhaps it is better so. Perhaps it is better that I should
carry with me a fond dream of what might have been, than to
have been told by you that such a dream could never come true.
I had intended to give you the highest evidence of my respect
and esteem that man can give to woman, but I have been over-
ruled by fate or circumstance. I shall love you as long as I
live. One thing more : should you ever find yourself in need
of the services of a friend, — a friend in whom you may place
the most implicit confidence, — send for Mr. Jack Walthall.
Say to him that Little Compton commended you to his care and
attention, and give him my love."

Walthall drew a long breath and threw his head
back as he finished reading this. Whatever emotion
he may have felt, he managed to conceal, but there
was a little color in his usually pale face, and his
dark eyes shone with a new light.

"This is a very unfortunate mistake," he exclaimed. "What is to be done?"

Miss Fairleigh smiled.

"There is no mistake, Mr. Walthall," she replied.

"Mr. Compton is a Northern man, and he has gone to join the Northern army. I think he is right."

"Well," said Walthall, "he will do what he thinks is right, but I wish he was here to-night."

"Oh, so do I!" exclaimed Miss Fairleigh, and then she blushed; seeing which, Mr. Jack Walthall drew his own conclusions.

"If I could get through the lines," she went on, "I would go home." Whereupon Walthall offered her all the assistance in his power, and offered to escort her to the Potomac. But before arrangements for the journey could be made, there came the news of the first battle of Manassas, and the conflict was begun in earnest; so earnest, indeed, that it changed the course of a great many lives, and gave even a new direction to American history.

Miss Fairleigh's friends in Hillsborough would not permit her to risk the journey through the lines; and Capt. Walthall's company was ordered to the front, where the young men composing it entered headlong into the hurly-burly that goes by the name of war.

There was one little episode growing out of Jack Walthall's visit to Miss Fairleigh that ought to be told. When that young gentleman bade her good-evening, and passed out of the parlor, Miss Fairleigh placed her hands to her face and fell to weeping, as women will.

Major Bass, sitting on the veranda, had been an interested spectator of the conference in the parlor, but it was in the nature of a pantomine. He could hear nothing that was said, but he could see that Miss Fairleigh and Walthall were both laboring under some strong excitement. When, therefore, he saw Walthall pass hurriedly out, leaving Miss Fairleigh in tears in the parlor, it occurred to him that, as the head of the household and the natural protector of the women under his roof, he was bound to take some action. He called Jesse, the negro house-servant, who was on duty in the dining-room.

"Jess! Jess! Oh, Jess!" There was an insinuating sweetness in his voice, as it echoed through the hall. Jesse, doubtless recognizing the velvety quality of the tone, made his appearance promptly. "Jess," said the major softly, "I wish you'd please fetch me my shot-gun. Make 'aste, Jess, and don't make no furse."

Jesse went after the shot-gun, and the major waddled into the parlor. He cleared his throat at the door, and Miss Fairleigh looked up.

"Miss Lizzie, did Jack Walthall insult you here in my house?"

"Insult me, sir! Why, he's the noblest gentleman alive."

The major drew a deep breath of relief, and smiled.

"Well, I'm mighty glad to hear you say so!" he exclaimed. "I couldn't tell, to save my life, what put it into my mind. Why, I might 'a' know'd that

Jack Walthall ain't that kind of a chap. Lord! I reckon I must be getting old and weak-minded. Don't cry no more, honey. Go right along and go to bed." As he turned to go out of the parlor, he was confronted by Jesse with the shot-gun. "Oh, go put her up, Jess," he said apologetically; "go put her up, boy. I wanted to blaze away at a dog out there trying to scratch under the palings; but the dog's done gone. Go put her up, Jess."

When Jess carried the gun back, he remarked casually to his mistress, —

"Miss Sa'h, you better keep yo' eye on Marse Maje. He talkin' mighty funny, en he doin' mighty quare."

Thereafter, for many a long day, the genial major sat in his cool veranda, and thought of Jack Walthall and the boys in Virginia. Sometimes between dozes he would make his way to Perdue's Corner, and discuss the various campaigns. How many desperate campaigns were fought on that Corner! All the older citizens, who found it convenient or necessary to stay at home, had in them the instinct and emotions of great commanders. They knew how victory could be wrung from defeat, and how success could be made more overwhelming. At Perdue's Corner, Washington City was taken not less than a dozen times a week, and occasionally both New York and Boston were captured and sacked. Of all the generals who fought their battles at the Corner, Major

Jimmy Bass was the most energetic, the most daring, and the most skilful. As a strategist he had no superior. He had a way of illustrating the feasibility of his plans by drawing them in the sand with his cane. Fat as he was, the major had a way of "surroundering" the enemy so that no avenue was left for his escape. At Perdue's Corner he captured Scott, and McClellan, and Joe Hooker, and John Pope, and held their entire forces as prisoners of war.

In spite of all this, however, the war went on. Sometimes word would come that one of the Hillsborough boys had been shot to death. Now and then one would come home with an arm or a leg missing; so that, before many months had passed, even the generals conducting their campaigns at Perdue's Corner managed to discover that war was a very serious business.

It happened that one day in July, Capt. Jack Walthall and his men, together with quite an imposing array of comrades, were called upon to breast the sultry thunder of Gettysburg. They bore themselves like men ; they went forward with a shout and a rush, facing the deadly slaughter of the guns ; they ran up the hill and to the rock wall. With others, Capt. Walthall leaped over the wall. They were met by a murderous fire that mowed down the men like grass. The line in the rear wavered, fell back, and went forward again. Capt. Walthall heard his name called in his front, and then some one cried, " Don't shoot ! " and Little Compton, his face blackened with powder, and his eyes glistening with excitement, rushed into Walthall's arms. The order not to shoot — if it was an order — came too late. There was another volley. As the Confederates rushed forward, the Federal line retreated a little way, and Walthall found himself surrounded by the small remnant of his men. The Confederates made one more effort to advance, but it was useless. The line was borne back, and finally retreated ; but when it went down the slope, Walthall and Lieut. Ransome had Little Compton between them. He was a prisoner. Just how it all happened, no one of the three could describe, but Little Compton was carried into the Confederate lines. He was wounded in the shoulder and in the arm, and the ball that shattered his arm shattered Walthall's arm.

They were carried to the field hospital, where Walthall insisted that Little Compton's wounds should be looked after first. The result was, that Walthall lost his left arm and Compton his right ; and then, when by some special interposition of Providence they escaped gangrene and other results of imperfect surgery and bad nursing, they went to Richmond, where Walthall's money and influence secured them comfortable quarters.

Hillsborough had heard of all this in a vague way, — indeed, a rumor of it had been printed in the

Rockville "Vade Mecum," — but the generals and commanders in consultation at Perdue's Corner were astonished one day when the stage-coach set down at the door of the tavern a tall, one-armed gentleman in gray, and a short, one-armed gentleman in blue.

"By the livin' Lord!" exclaimed Major Jimmy Bass, "if that ain't Jack Walthall! And you may put out my two eyes if that ain't Little Compton! Why, shucks, boys!" he exclaimed, as he waddled across the street, "I'd 'a' know'd you anywheres. I'm a little short-sighted, and I'm mighty nigh took off wi' the dropsy, but I'd 'a' know'd you anywheres."

There were handshakings and congratulations from everybody in the town. The clerks and the merchants deserted their stores to greet the new-comers, and there seemed to be a general jubilee. For weeks Capt. Jack Walthall was compelled to tell his Gettysburg story over and over again, frequently to the same hearers ; and, curiously enough, there was never a murmur of dissent when he told how Little Compton had insisted on wearing his Federal uniform.

"Great Jiminy Craminy!" Major Jimmy Bass would exclaim ; "don't we all know Little Compton like a book ? And ain't he got a right to wear his own duds ? "

Rockville, like every other railroad town in the

South at that period, had become the site of a Confederate hospital ; and sometimes the hangers-on and
convalescents paid brief visits of inspection to the
neighboring villages.   On one occasion a little squad
of them made their appearance on the streets of
Hillsborough, and made a good-natured attempt to
fraternize with the honest citizens who gathered
daily at Perdue's Corner.   While they were thus
engaged, Little Compton, arrayed in his blue uniform, passed down the street.   The visitors made
some inquiries, and Major Bass gave them a very
sympathetic history of Little Compton.   Evidently
they failed to appreciate the situation ; for one of
them, a tall Mississippian, stretched himself and
remarked to his companions, —

"Boys, when we go, we'll just about lift that feller
and take him along.   He belongs in Andersonville,
that's where he belongs."

Major Bass looked at the tall Mississippian and
smiled.

"I reckon you must 'a' been mighty sick over
yander," said the major, indicating Rockville.

"Well, yes," said the Mississippian ; "I've had
a pretty tough time."

"And you ain't strong yet," the major went on.

"Well, I'm able to get about right lively," said the
other.

"Strong enough to go to war ? "

"Oh, well, not — not just yet."

"Well, then," said the major in his bluntest tone, "you better be mighty keerful of yourself in this town. If you ain't strong enough to go to war, you better let Little Compton alone."

The tall Mississippian and his friends took the hint, and Little Compton continued to wear his blue uniform unmolested. About this time Atlanta fell; and there were vague rumors in the air, chiefly among the negroes, that Sherman's army would march down and capture Hillsborough, which, by the assembly of generals at Perdue's Corner, was regarded as a strategic point. These vague rumors proved to be correct; and by the time the first frosts fell, Perdue's Corner had reason to believe that Gen. Sherman was marching down on Hillsborough. Dire rumors of fire, rapine, and pillage preceded the approach of the Federal army, and it may well be supposed that these rumors spread consternation in the air. Major Bass professed to believe that Gen. Sherman would be "surroundered" and captured before his troops reached Middle Georgia; but the three columns, miles apart, continued their march unopposed.

It was observed that during this period of doubt, anxiety, and terror, Little Compton was on the alert. He appeared to be nervous and restless. His conduct was so peculiar that some of the more suspicious citizens of the region predicted that he had been playing the part of a spy, and that he was merely waiting for the advent of Sherman's army in order to point out where his acquaintances had concealed their treasures.

One fine morning a company of Federal troopers rode into Hillsborough. They were met by Little Compton, who had borrowed one of Jack Walthall's horses for just such an occasion. The cavalcade paused in the public square, and, after a somewhat prolonged consultation with Little Compton, rode on in the direction of Rockville. During the day small parties of foragers made their appearance. Little Compton had some trouble with these; but, by hurrying hither and thither, he managed to prevent any depredations. He even succeeded in convincing the majority of them that they owed some sort of respect to that small town. There was one obstinate fellow, however, who seemed determined to prosecute his search for valuables. He was a German who evidently did not understand English.

In the confusion Little Compton lost sight of the German, though he had determined to keep an eye on him. It was not long before he heard of him again; for one of the Walthall negroes came running across the public square, showing by voice and gesture that he was very much alarmed.

"Marse Compton! Marse Compton!" he cried, "you better run up ter Marse Jack's, kaze one er dem mens is gwine in dar whar ole Miss is, en ef he do dat he gwine ter git hurted!"

Little Compton hurried to the Walthall place, and

he was just in time to see Jack rushing the German
down the wide flight of steps that led to the veranda.
What might have happened, no one can say; what
did happen may be briefly told. The German, his
face inflamed with passion, had seized his gun, which
had been left outside, and was aiming at Jack Walthall, who stood on the steps, cool and erect. An
exclamation of mingled horror and indignation from
Little Compton attracted the German's attention, and
caused him to turn his head. This delay probably
saved Jack Walthall's life; for the German, thinking
that a comrade was coming to his aid, levelled his
gun again and fired. But Little Compton had seized
the weapon near the muzzle and wrested it around.
The bullet, instead of reaching its target, tore its way
through Compton's empty sleeve. In another instant
the German was covered by Compton's revolver.
The hand that held it was steady, and the eyes that
glanced along its shining barrel fairly blazed. The
German dropped his gun. All trace of passion disappeared from his face; and presently seeing that
the crisis had passed, so far as he was concerned, he
wheeled in his tracks, gravely saluted Little Compton,
and made off at a double-quick.

"You musn't think hard of the boys, Jack, on
account of that chap. They understand the whole
business, and they are going to take care of this
town."

And they did. The army came marching along

presently, and the stragglers found Hillsborough pa-
trolled by a detachment of cavalry. Walthall and
Little Compton stood on the wide steps, and reviewed
this imposing array as it passed before them. The
tall Confederate, in his uniform of gray, rested his
one hand affectionately on the shoulder of the stout
little man in blue, and on the bosom of each was
pinned an empty sleeve. Unconsciously, they made
an impressive picture. The Commander, grim, gray,
and resolute, observed it with sparkling eyes. The
spectacle was so unusual — so utterly opposed to the
logic of events — that he stopped with his staff long
enough to hear Little Compton tell his story. He
was a grizzled, aggressive man, this Commander, but
his face lighted up wonderfully at the recital.

"Well, you know this sort of thing doesn't end
the war, boys," he said, as he shook hands with
Walthall and Little Compton ; "but I shall sleep
better to-night."

Perhaps he did. Perhaps he dreamed that what
he had seen and heard was prophetic of the days to
come, when peace and fraternity should seize upon
the land, and bring unity, happiness, and prosperity
to the people.

AUNT FOUNTAIN'S PRISONER.

IT is curious how the smallest incident, the most
unimportant circumstance, will recall old friends
and old associations. An old gentleman, who is
noted far and near for his prodigious memory of
dates and events, once told me that his memory,
so astonishing to his friends and acquaintances, consisted not so much in remembering names and dates
and facts, as in associating each of these with some
special group of facts and events; so that he always
had at command a series of associations to which he
could refer instantly and confidently. This is an
explanation of the system of employing facts, but not
of the method by which they are accumulated and
stored away.

I was reminded of this some years ago by a paragraph in one of the county newspapers that sometimes come under my observation. It was a very
commonplace paragraph; indeed, it was in the nature
of an advertisement, — an announcement of the fact
that orders for "gilt-edged butter" from the Jersey
farm on the Tomlinson Place should be left at the
drug-store in Rockville, where the first that came
would be the first served. This business-like notice

was signed by Ferris Trunion. The name was not only peculiar, but new to me; but this was of no importance at all. The fact that struck me was the bald and bold announcement that the Tomlinson Place was the site and centre of trading and other commercial transactions in butter. I can only imagine what effect this announcement would have had on my grandmother, who died years ago, and on some other old people I used to know. Certainly they would have been horrified; and no wonder, for when they were in their prime the Tomlinson Place was the seat of all that was high, and mighty, and grand, in the social world in the neighborhood of Rockville. I remember that everybody stood in awe of the Tomlinsons. Just why this was so, I never could make out. They were very rich; the Place embraced several thousand acres; but if the impressions made on me when a child are worth any thing, they were extremely simple in their ways. Though, no doubt, they could be formal and conventional enough when occasion required.

I have no distinct recollection of Judge Addison Tomlinson, except that he was a very tall old gentleman, much older than his wife, who went about the streets of Rockville carrying a tremendous gold-headed cane carved in a curious manner. In those days I knew more of Mrs. Tomlinson than I did of the judge, mainly because I heard a great deal more about her. Some of the women called her Mrs.

Judge Tomlinson ; but my grandmother never called her any thing else but Harriet Bledsoe, which was her maiden name. It was a name, too, that seemed to suit her, so that when you once heard her called Harriet Bledsoe, you never forgot it afterward. I do not know now, any more than I did when a child, why this particular name should fit her so exactly ; but, as I have often been told, a lack of knowledge does not alter facts.

I think my grandmother used to go to church to see what kind of clothes Harriet Bledsoe wore ; for I have often heard her say, after the sermon was over, that Harriet's bonnet, or Harriet's dress, was perfectly charming. Certainly Mrs. Tomlinson was always dressed in the height of fashion, though it was a very simple fashion when compared with the flounces and furbelows of her neighbors. I remem- ber this distinctly, that she seemed to be perfectly cool the hottest Sunday in summer, and comfortably warm the coldest Sunday in winter ; and I am con- vinced that this impression, made on the mind of a child, must bear some definite relation to Mrs. Tomlinson's good taste.

Certainly my grandmother was never tired of tell- ing me that Harriet Bledsoe was blessed with excep- tionally good taste and fine manners ; and I remember that she told me often how she wished I was a girl, so that I might one day be in a position to take ad- vantage of the opportunities I had had of profiting by

Harriet Bledsoe's example. I think there was some sort of attachment between my grandmother and Mrs. Tomlinson, formed when they were at school together, though my grandmother was much the older of the two. But there was no intimacy. The gulf that money sometimes makes between those who have it and those who lack it lay between them. Though I think my grandmother was more sensitive about crossing this gulf than Mrs. Tomlinson.

I was never in the Tomlinson house but once when a child. Whether it was because it was two or three miles away from Rockville, or whether it was because I stood in awe of my grandmother's Harriet Bledsoe, I do not know. But I have a very vivid recollection of the only time I went there as a boy. One of my playmates, a rough-and-tumble little fellow, was sent by his mother, a poor sick woman, to ask Mrs. Tomlinson for some preserves. I think this woman and her little boy were in some way related to the Tomlinsons. The richest and most powerful people, I have heard it said, are not so rich and powerful but they are pestered by poor kin, and the Tomlinsons were no exception to the rule.

I went with this little boy I spoke of, and I was afraid afterward that I was in some way responsible for his boldness. He walked right into the presence of Mrs. Tomlinson, and, without waiting to return the lady's salutation, he said in a loud voice, —

"Aunt Harriet, ma says send her some of your nicest preserves."

"*Aunt Harriet*, indeed!" she exclaimed, and then she gave him a look that was cold enough to freeze him, and hard enough to send him through the floor.

I think she relented a little, for she went to one of the windows, bigger than any door you see nowadays, and looked out over the blooming orchard; and then after a while she came back to us, and was very gracious. She patted me on the head; and I must have shrunk from her touch, for she laughed and said she never bit nice little boys. Then she asked me my name; and when I told her, she said my grandmother was the dearest woman in the world. Moreover, she told my companion that it would spoil preserves to carry them about in a tin bucket; and then she fetched a big basket, and had it filled with preserves, and jelly, and cake. There were some ginger-preserves among the rest, and I remember that I appreciated them very highly; the more so, since my companion had a theory of his own that ginger-preserves and fruit-cake were not good for sick people.

I remember, too, that Mrs. Tomlinson had a little daughter about my own age. She had long yellow hair and very black eyes. She rode around in the Tomlinson carriage a great deal, and everybody said she was remarkably pretty, with a style and a spirit

all her own.   The negroes used to say that she was
as affectionate as she was wilful, which was saying
a good deal.   It was characteristic of Harriet Bledsoe, my grandmother said, that her little girl should
be named Lady.

I heard a great many of the facts I have stated
from old Aunt Fountain, one of the Tomlinson
negroes, who, for some reason or other, was permitted to sell ginger-cakes and persimmon-beer under
the wide-spreading China-trees in Rockville on public days and during court-week.   There was a theory
among certain envious people in Rockville, — there
are envious people everywhere, — that the Tomlinsons, notwithstanding the extent of their landed
estate and the number of their negroes, were sometimes short of ready cash ; and it was hinted that
they pocketed the proceeds of Aunt Fountain's persimmon-beer and ginger-cakes.   Undoubtedly such
stories as these were the outcome of pure envy.
When my grandmother heard such gossip as this,
she sighed, and said that people who would talk
about Harriet Bledsoe in that way would talk about
anybody under the sun.   My own opinion is, that
Aunt Fountain got the money and kept it ; otherwise she would not have been so fond of her master
and mistress, nor so proud of the family and its
position.   I spent many an hour near Aunt Fountain's cake and beer stand, for I liked to hear her
talk.   Besides, she had a very funny name, and I

thought there was always a probability that she
would explain how she got it.   But she never did.

I had forgotten all about the Tomlinsons until the
advertisement I have mentioned was accidentally
brought to my notice, whereupon memory suddenly
became wonderfully active.   I am keenly alive to
the happier results of the war, and I hope I appreciate at their full value the emancipation of both
whites and blacks from the deadly effects of negro
slavery, and the wonderful development of our mate-
rial resources that the war has rendered possible ;
but I must confess it was with a feeling of regret that
I learned that the Tomlinson Place had been turned
into a dairy-farm.   Moreover, the name of Ferris
Trunion had a foreign and an unfamiliar sound.
His bluntly worded advertisement appeared to come
from the mind of a man who would not hesitate to
sweep away both romance and tradition if they happened to stand in the way of a profitable bargain.

I was therefore much gratified, some time after
reading Trunion's advertisement, to receive a note
from a friend who deals in real estate, telling me
that some land near the Tomlinson Place had been
placed in his hands for sale, and asking me to go to
Rockville to see if the land and the situation were
all they were described to be.   I lost no time in
undertaking this part of the business, for I was
anxious to see how the old place looked in the hands
of strangers, and unsympathetic strangers at that.

It is not far from Atlanta to Rockville, — a day
and a night, — and the journey is not fatiguing ; so
that a few hours after receiving my friend's request
I was sitting in the veranda of the Rockville Hotel,
observing, with some degree of wonder, the vast
changes that had taken place — the most of them for
the better. There were new faces and new enterprises all around me, and there was a bustle about
the town that must have caused queer sensations
in the minds of the few old citizens who still gathered
at the post-office for the purpose of carrying on
ancient political controversies with each other.

Among the few familiar figures that attracted my
attention was that of Aunt Fountain. The old
China-tree in the shade of which she used to sit had
been blasted by lightning or fire ; but she still had
her stand there, and she was keeping the flies and
dust away with the same old turkey-tail fan. I
could see no change. If her hair was grayer, it was
covered and concealed from view by the snow-white
handkerchief tied around her head. From my place
I could hear her humming a tune, — the tune I had
heard her sing in precisely the same way years ago.
I heard her scolding a little boy. The gesture, the
voice, the words, were the same she had employed
in trying to convince me that my room was much
better than my company, especially in the neighborhood of her cake-stand. To see and hear her thus
gave me a peculiar feeling of homesickness. I

approached and saluted her. She bowed with old-fashioned politeness, but without looking up.

"De biggest uns, dee er ten cent," she said, pointing to her cakes; "en de littlest, dee er fi' cent. I make um all myse'f, suh. En de beer in dat jug — dat beer got body, suh."

"I have eaten many a one of your cakes, Aunt Fountain," said I, "and drank many a glass of your beer; but you have forgotten me."

"My eye weak, suh, but dee ain' weak nuff fer dat." She shaded her eyes with her fan, and looked at me. Then she rose briskly from her chair. "De Lord he'p my soul!" she exclaimed enthusiastically. "W'y, I know you w'en you little boy. W'at make I ain' know you w'en you big man? My eye weak, suh, but dee ain' weak nuff fer dat. Well, suh, you mus' eat some my ginger-cake. De Lord know you has make way wid um w'en you wuz little boy."

The invitation was accepted, but somehow the ginger-cakes had lost their old-time relish; in me the taste and spirit of youth were lacking.

We talked of old times and old friends, and I told Aunt Fountain that I had come to Rockville for the purpose of visiting in the neighborhood of the Tomlinson Place.

"Den I gwine wid you, suh," she cried, shaking her head vigorously. "I gwine wid you." And go she did.

"I been layin' off ter go see my young mistiss dis

long time," said Aunt Fountain, the next day, after we had started. "I glad I gwine deer in style. De niggers won' know me skacely, ridin' in de buggy dis away."

"Your young mistress?" I inquired.

"Yes, suh. You know Miss Lady w'en she little gal. She grown oman now."

"Well, who is this Trunion I have heard of?"

"He monst'ous nice w'ite man, suh. He married my young mistiss. He monst'ous nice w'ite man."

"But who is he? Where did he come from?"

Aunt Fountain chuckled convulsively as I asked these questions.

"We-all des pick 'im up, suh. Yes, suh; we-all des pick 'im up. Ain' you year talk 'bout dat, suh? I dunner whar you bin at ef you ain' never is year talk 'bout dat. He de fus' w'ite man w'at I ever pick up, suh. Yes, suh; de ve'y fus' one."

"I don't understand you," said I; "tell me about it."

At this Aunt Fountain laughed long and loudly. She evidently enjoyed my ignorance keenly.

"De Lord know I oughtn' be laughin' like dis. I ain' laugh so hearty sence I wuz little gal mos', en dat wuz de time w'en Marse Rowan Tomlinson come 'long en ax me my name. I tell 'im, I did, 'I'm name Flew Ellen, suh.' Marse Rowan he deaf ez any dead hoss. He 'low, 'Hey?' I say, 'I'm name Flew Ellen, suh.' Marse Rowan say, 'Fountain! Huh! he quare name.' I holler en laugh, en w'en de folks ax me w'at I hollerin' 'bout, I tell um dat Marse Rowan say I'm name Fountain. Well, suh, fum dat day down ter dis, stedder Flew Ellen, I'm bin name Fountain. I laugh hearty den en my name got change, en I feared ef I laugh now de hoss'll run away en turn de buggy upperside down right spang on top er me."

"But about this Mr. Trunion?" said I.

"Name er de Lord!" exclaimed Aunt Fountain, ain' you never is bin year 'bout dat? You bin mighty fur ways, suh, kaze we all bin knowin' 'bout it fum de jump."

"No doubt. Now tell me about it."

Aunt Fountain shook her head, and her face assumed a serious expression.

"I dunno 'bout dat, suh. I year tell dat niggers ain' got no business fer go talkin' 'bout fambly doin's. Yit dar wuz yo' gran'mammy. My mistiss sot lots by her, en you been bornded right yer 'long wid um. I don't speck it'll be gwine so mighty fur out'n de fambly ef I tell you 'bout it."

I made no attempt to coax Aunt Fountain to tell me about Trunion, for I knew it would be difficult to bribe her not to talk about him. She waited a while, evidently to tease my curiosity; but as I betrayed none, and even made an effort to talk about something else, she began: —

"Well, suh, you ax me 'bout Marse Fess Trunion.

I know you bleeze ter like dat man.   He ain' b'long ter we-all folks, no furder dan he my young mistiss ole man, but dee ain' no finer w'ite man dan him. No, suh; dee ain'.   I tell you dat p'intedly.   De niggers, dee say he mighty close en pinchin', but deze is mighty pinchin' times — you know dat yo'se'f, suh.   Ef a man don' fa'rly fling 'way he money, dem Tomlinson niggers, dee'll say he mighty pinchin'.   I hatter be pinchin' myse'f, suh, kaze I know time I sell my ginger-cakes dat ef I don't grip onter de money, dee won' be none lef' fer buy flour en 'lasses fer make mo'.   It de Lord's trufe, suh, kaze I done had trouble dat way many's de time.   I say dis 'bout Marse Fess Trunion, ef he ain' got de blood, he got de breedin'.   Ef he ain' good ez de Tomlinsons, he lots better dan some folks w'at I know."

I gathered from all this that Trunion was a foreigner of some kind, but I found out my mistake later.

"I pick dat man up myse'f, en I knows 'im 'most good ez ef he wuz one er we-all."

"What do you mean when you say 'you picked him up'?" I asked, unable to restrain my impatience.

"Well, suh, de fus' time I see Marse Fess Trunion wuz terreckerly atter de Sherman army come 'long.   Dem wuz hot times, suh, col' ez de wedder wuz.   Dee wuz in-about er million un um

look like ter me, en dee des ravage de face er de
yeth.   Dee tuck all de hosses, en all de cows, en all
de chickens.   Yes, suh; dee cert'n'y did.   Man
come 'long, en 'low, 'Aunty, you free now,' en den
he tuck all my ginger-cakes w'at I bin bakin' 'g'inst
Chris'mus; en den I say, 'Ef I wuz free ez you is,
suh, I'd fling you down en take dem ginger-cakes
'way fum you.'   Yes, suh.   I tole 'im dat.   It make
me mad fer see de way dat man walk off wid my
ginger-cakes.

"I got so mad, suh, dat I foller 'long atter him
little ways; but dat ain' do no good, kaze he come
ter whar dee wuz some yuther men, en dee 'vide up
dem cakes till dee want no cake lef'.   Den I struck
'cross de plan'ation, en walked 'bout in de drizzlin'
rain tell I cool off my madness, suh, kaze de flour
dat went in dem cakes cos' me mos' a hunderd dollars in good Confederick money.   Yes, suh; it did
dat.   En I work for dat money mighty hard.

"Well, suh, I ain' walk fur 'fo' it seem like I year
some un talkin'.   I stop, I did, en lissen, en still I
year um.   I ain' see nobody, suh, but still I year
um.   I walk fus' dis away en den dat away, en den
I walk 'roun' en 'roun', en den it pop in my min'
'bout de big gully.   It ain' dar now, suh, but in dem
days we call it de big gully, kaze it wuz wide en deep.
Well, suh,' fo' I git dar I see hoss-tracks, en dee led
right up ter de brink.   I look in, I did, en down dar
dee wuz a man en a hoss.   Yes, suh; dee wuz bofe

down dar. De man wuz layin' out flat on he back,
en de hoss he wuz layin' sorter up en down de
gully en right on top er one er de man legs, en
eve'y time de hoss'd scramble en try fer git up de
man 'ud talk at 'im. I know dat hoss mus' des
nata'lly a groun' dat man legs in de yeth, suh. Yes,
suh. It make my flesh crawl w'en I look at um.
Yit de man ain' talk like he mad. No, suh, he
ain'; en it make me feel like somebody done gone
en hit me on de funny-bone w'en I year 'im talkin'
dat away. Eve'y time de hoss scuffle, de man he
'low, 'Hol' up, ole fel, you er mashin' all de shape
out'n me.' Dat w'at he say, suh. En den he 'low,
'Ef you know how you hurtin', ole fel, I des know
you'd be still.' Yes, suh. Dem he ve'y words.

"All dis time de rain wuz a-siftin' down. It fall
mighty saft, but 'twuz monst'ous wet, suh. Bimeby
I crope up nigher de aidge, en w'en de man see me
he holler out, 'Hol' on, aunty; don't you fall down
yer!'

"I ax 'im, I say, 'Marster, is you hurted much?'
Kaze time I look at 'im I know he ain' de villyun
w'at make off wid my ginger-cakes. Den he 'low,
'I speck I hurt purty bad, aunty, en de wuss un it is
dat my hoss keep hurtin' me mo'.'

"Den nex' time de hoss move it errortate me so,
suh, dat I holler at 'im loud ez I ken, 'Wo dar, you
scan'lous villyun! Wo!' Well, suh, I speck dat
hoss mus a-bin use'n ter niggers, kaze time I holler

at 'im he lay right still, suh. I slid down dat bank, en I kotch holter dat bridle — I don't look like I'm mighty strong, does I, suh?" said Aunt Fountain, pausing suddenly in her narrative to ask the question.

"Well, no," said I, humoring her as much as possible. "You don't seem to be as strong as some people I've seen."

"Dat's it, suh!" she exclaimed. "Dat w'at worry me. I slid down dat bank, en I kotch dat hoss by de bridle. De man say, 'Watch out dar, aunty! don't let he foot hit you. Dee one cripple too much now.' I ain' pay no 'tention, suh. I des grab de bridle, en I slew dat hoss head roun', en I fa'rly lif' 'im on he foots. Yes, suh, I des lif' 'im on he foots. Den I led 'im down de gully en turnt 'im a-loose, en you ain' never see no hoss supjued like dat hoss wuz, suh. Den I went back whar de man layin', en ax 'im ef he feel better, en he' low dat he feel like he got a big load lif' offen he min', en den, mos' time he say dat, suh, he faint dead away. Yes, suh. He des faint dead away. I ain' never is see no man like dat, w'at kin be jokin' one minnit en den de nex' be dead, ez you may say. But dat's Marse Fess Trunion, suh. Dat's him up en down.

"Well, suh, I stan' dar, I did, en I ain' know w'at in de name er de Lord I gwine do. I wuz des ez wringin' wet ez if I'd a-bin baptize in de water; en de man he wuz mo' wetter dan w'at I wuz, en good-

ness knows how long he bin layin' dar. I run back
ter de big-'ouse, suh, mighty nigh a mile, en I done
my level bes' fer fin' some er de niggers en git um
fer go wid me back dar en git de man. But I ain'
fin' none un um, suh. Dem w'at ain' gone wid de
Sherman army, dee done hide out. Den I went in
de big-ouse, suh, en tell Mistiss 'bout de man down
dar in de gully, en how he done hurted so bad he
ain' kin walk. Den Mistiss — I speck you done fergit Mistiss, suh — Mistiss, she draw herse'f up en
ax w'at business dat man er any yuther man got on
her plan'ation. I say, 'Yassum, dat so; but he done
dar, en ef he stay dar he gwine die dar.' Yes, suh;
dat w'at I say. I des put it at Mistiss right pine-
blank.

"Den my young mistiss — dat's Miss Lady, suh —
she say dat dough she spize um all dez bad az she
kin, dat man mus' be brung away from dar. Kaze,
she say, she don't keer how yuther folks go on, de
Tomlinsons is bleeze to do like Christun people.
Yes, suh; she say dem ve'y words. Den Mistiss,
she 'low dat de man kin be brung up, en put in de
corn-crib, but Miss Lady she say no, he mus' be
brung en put right dar in de big 'ouse in one er de
up-sta'rs rooms, kaze maybe some er dem State er
Georgy boys mought be hurted up dar in de Norf,
en want some place fer stay at. Yes, suh; dat des
de way she talk. Den Mistiss, she ain' say nothin',
yit she hol' her head mighty high.

"Well, suh, I went back out in de yard, en den
I went 'cross ter de nigger-quarter, en I ain' gone
fur tell I year my ole man prayin' in dar some'r's.
I know 'im by he v'ice, suh, en he wuz prayin' des
like it wuz camp-meetin' time.   I hunt 'roun' fer 'im,
suh, en bimeby I fin' 'im squattin' down behime de
do'.   I grab 'im, I did, en I shuck 'im, en I 'low,
'Git up fum yer, you nasty, stinkin' ole villyun, you!'
Yes, suh ; I wuz mad.   I say, 'W'at you doin' squattin' down on de flo'?   Git up fum dar en come go
'long wid me!'   I hatter laugh, suh, kaze w'en I
shuck my ole man by de shoulder, en holler at 'im,
he put up he two han', suh, en squall out, 'Oh, pray
marster! don't kill me dis time, en I ain' never
gwine do it no mo'!'

"Atter he 'come pacify, suh, den I tell him 'bout
de man down dar in de gully, en yit we ain' know
w'at ter do.   My ole man done hide out some er de
mules en hosses down in de swamp, en he feard ter
go atter um, suh, kaze he skeerd de Sherman army
would come marchin' back en fine um, en he 'low
dat he mos' know dee er comin' back atter dat man
down dar.   Yes, suh ; he de skeerdest nigger w'at
I ever see, if I do say it myse'f.   Yit, bimeby he
put out atter one er de hosses, en he brung 'im back ;
en we hitch 'im up in de spring-waggin, en atter dat
man we went.   Yes, suh ; we did dat.   En w'en we
git dar, dat ar man wuz plum ravin' deestracted.   He
wuz laughin' en talkin' wid hese'f, en gwine on, tell

it make yo' blood run col' fer lissen at 'im. Yes, suh.

"Me en my ole man, we pick 'im up des like he wuz baby. I come mighty nigh droppin' 'im, suh, kaze one time, wiles we kyarn 'im up de bank, I year de bones in he leg rasp up 'g'inst one er n'er. Yes, suh. It make me blin' sick, suh. We kyard 'im home en put 'im up st'ars, en dar he stayed fer many's de long day."

"Where was Judge Tomlinson?" I asked. At this Aunt Fountain grew more serious than ever, — a seriousness that was expressed by an increased particularity and emphasis in both speech and manner.

"You axin' 'bout Marster? Well, suh, he wuz dar. He wuz cert'n'y dar wid Mistiss en Miss Lady, suh, but look like he ain' take no intruss in w'at gwine on. *Some* folks 'low, suh, dat he ain' right in he head, but dee ain' know 'im — dee ain' know 'im, suh, like we-all. Endurin' er de war, suh, he wuz strucken wid de polzy, en den w'en he git well, he ain' take no intruss in w'at gwine on. Dey'd be long days, suh, w'en he ain' take no notice er nobody ner nuttin' but Miss Lady. He des had dem spells; en den, ag'in, he'd set out on de peazzer en sing by hese'f, en it make me feel so lonesome dat I bleeze ter cry. Yes, suh; it's de Lord's trufe.

"Well, suh, dat man w'at I fin' out dar in de gully wuz Marse Fess Trunion. Yes, suh, de ve'y same man. Dee ain' no tellin' w'at dat po' creetur gone

thoo wid. He had fever, he had pneumony, en he
had dat broke leg. En all 'long wid dat dee want
skacely no time w'en he want laughin' en jokin'.
Our w'ite folks, dee des spized 'im kase he bin wid
Sherman army. Dee say he wuz Yankee; but I tell
um, suh, dat ef Yankee look dat away dee wuz
cert'n'y mighty like we-all. Mistiss, she ain' never
go 'bout 'im wiles he sick; en Miss Lady, she keep
mighty shy, en she tu'n up her nose eve'y time she
year 'im laugh. Oh, yes, suh; dee cert'n'y spize de
Yankees endurin' er dem times. Dee hated um
rank, suh. I tell um, I say, ' You-all des wait. Dee
ain' no nicer man dan w'at he is, en you-all des
wait tell you know 'im.' *Shoo!* I des might ez well
talk ter de win', suh, — dee hate de Yankees dat
rank.

"By de time dat man git so he kin creep 'bout
on crutches, he look mos' good ez he do now. He
wuz dat full er life, suh, dat he bleeze ter go down-
sta'rs, en down he went. Well, suh, he wuz mighty
lucky dat day. Kase ef he'd a run up wid Mistiss en
Miss Lady by hese'f, dec'd er done sumpn' ner fer
ter make 'im feel bad. Dee cert'n'y would, suh.
But dee wuz walkin' 'roun' in de yard, en he come
out on de peazzer whar Marster wuz sunnin' hese'f
and singin'. I wouldn' b'lieve it, suh, ef I ain' see
it wid my two eyes; but Marster got up out'n he
cheer, en straighten hese'f, en shuck han's wid Mars
Fess, en look like he know all 'bout it. Dee sot dar,

suh, en talk en laugh, en laugh en talk, tell bimeby
I 'gun ter git skeerd on de accounts er bofe un um.
Dee talk 'bout de war, en dee talk 'bout de Yankees,
en dee talk politics right straight 'long des like
Marster done 'fo' he bin strucken wid de polzy.
En he talk sense, suh. He cert'n'y did. Bimeby
Mistiss en Miss Lady come back fum dee walk, en
dee look like dee gwine drap w'en dee see w'at
gwine on. Dem two mens wuz so busy talkin', suh,
dat dee ain' see de wimmen folks, en dee des keep
right on wid dee argafyin'. Mistiss en Miss Lady,
dee ain' know w'at ter make er all dis, en dee stan'
dar lookin' fus' at Marster en den at one er n'er.
Bimeby dee went up de steps en start to go by, but
Marster he riz up en stop um. Yes, suh. He riz
right up en stop um, en right den en dar, suh, he
make um interjuced ter one an'er. He stan' up, en
he say, 'Mr. Trunion, dis my wife; Mr. Trunion,
dis my daughter.'

"Well, suh, I wuz stannin' back in de big hall, en
we'n I see Marster gwine on dat away my knees
come mighty nigh failin' me, suh. Dis de fus' time
w'at he reckermember anybody name, an de fus'
time he do like he useter, sence he bin sick wid de
polzy. Mistiss en Miss Lady, dee come 'long in
atter w'ile, en dee look like dee skeerd. Well, suh,
I des far'ly preach at um. Yes, suh; I did dat. I
say, 'You see dat? You see how Marster doin'?
Ef de han' er de Lord ain' in dat, den he han' ain'

bin in nuttin' on de top side er dis yeth.' I say,
'You see how you bin cuttin' up 'roun' dat sick
w'ite man wid yo' biggity capers, en yit de Lord
retch down en make Marster soun' en well time de
yuther w'ite man tetch 'im.' Well, suh, dey wuz dat
worked up dat dey sot down en cried. Yes, suh;
dey did dat. Dey cried. En I ain' tellin' you no lie,
suh, I stood dar en cried wid um. Let 'lone dat,
I des far'ly boohooed. Yes, suh; dat's me. W'en I
git ter cryin' sho' nuff, I bleeze ter boohoo.

  " Fum dat on, Marster do like hese'f, en talk like
hese'f. It look like he bin sleep long time, suh, en
de sleep done 'im good. All he sense come back;
en you know, suh, de Tomlinsons, w'en dey at
deese'f, got much sense ez dee want en some fer
give way. Mistiss and Miss Lady, dee wuz mighty
proud 'bout Marster, suh, but dee ain' fergit dat de
yuther man wuz Yankee, en dee hol' deese'f monst'ous stiff. He notice dat hese'f, en he want ter
go 'way, but Marster, he 'fuse ter lissen at 'im right
pine-plank, suh. He say de dead Tomlinsons would
in-about turn over in dee graves ef dee know he sont
a cripple man 'way from he 'ouse. Den he want ter
pay he board, but Marster ain' lissen ter dat, en
needer is Mistiss; en dis mighty funny, too, kaze
right dat minnit dee want a half er dollar er good
money in de whole fambly, ceppin' some silver w'at
I work fer, en w'at I hide in er chink er my chimbly.
No, suh. Dee want er half er dollar in de whole

fambly, suh.   En yit dee won't take de greenbacks w'at dat man offer um.

"By dat time, suh, de war wuz done done, en dee wuz tough times.   Dee cert'n'y wuz, suh.   De rail-roads wuz all broke up, en eve'y thing look like it gwine helter-skelter right straight ter de Ole Boy. Dey want no law, suh, en dey want no nuttin'; en ef it hadn't er bin fer me en my ole man, I speck de Tomlinsons, proud ez dee wuz, would er bin mightily pincht fer fin' bread en meat.   But dee ain' never want fer it yit, suh, kaze w'en me en my ole man git whar we can't move no furder, Marse Fess Trunion, he tuck holt er de place en he fetcht it right side up terreckerly.   He say ter me dat he gwine pay he board dat away, suh, but he ain' say it whar de Tomlinsons kin year 'im, kaze den dee'd a-bin a fuss, suh.   But he kotch holt, en me, en him, en my ole man, we des he't eve'y thing hot.   Mo' speshually Marse Fess Trunion, suh.   You ain' know 'im, suh, but dat ar w'ite man, he got mo' ways ter work, en mo' short cuts ter de ways, suh, dan any w'ite man w'at I ever see, en I done see lots un um.   It got so, suh, dat me en my ole man ain' have ter draw no mo' rashuns fum de F'eedman Bureau; but dee wuz one spell, suh, w'en wuss rashuns dan dem wuz on de Tomlinson table.

"Well, suh, dat w'ite man, he work en he scuffle; he hire niggers, and he turn um off; he plan, en he projick; en 'tain' so mighty long, suh, 'fo' he got

eve'y thing gwine straight. How he done it, I'll
never tell you, suh; but do it he did. He put he
own money in dar, suh, kaze dee wuz two times dat I
knows un w'en he git money out'n de pos'-office, en
I see 'im pay it out ter de niggers, suh. En all dat
time he look like he de happies' w'ite man on top er
de groun', suh. Yes, suh. En w'en he at de 'ouse
Marster stuck right by 'im, en ef he bin he own son
he couldn't pay him mo' 'tention. Dee wuz times,
suh, w'en it seem like ter me dat Marse Fess Trunion
wuz a-cuttin' he eye at Miss Lady, en den I 'low
ter myse'f, 'Shoo, man! you mighty nice en all dat,
but you Yankee, en you nee'nter be a-drappin' yo'
wing 'roun' Miss Lady, kaze she too high-strung fer
dat.'

"It look like he see it de same way I do, suh, kaze
atter he git eve'y thing straight he say he gwine
home. Marster look like he feel mighty bad, but
Mistiss en Miss Lady, dee ain' say nuttin' 'tall. Den,
atter w'ile, suh, Marse Fess Trunion fix up, en off he
put. Yes, suh. He went off whar he come fum, en
I speck he folks wuz mighty glad ter see 'im atter so
long, kaze ef dee ever wuz a plum nice man it wuz
dat man. He want no great big man, suh, en he ain'
make much fuss, yit he lef' a mighty big hole at de
Tomlinson Place w'en he pulled out fum dar. Yes,
suh; he did dat. It look like it lonesome all over de
plan'ation. Marster, he' gun ter git droopy, but eve'y
time de dinner-bell ring he go ter de foot er de sta'rs

en call out, 'Come on, Trunion!' Yes, suh. He holler dat out eve'y day, en den, wiles he be talkin', he'd stop en look roun' en say, 'Whar Trunion?' It ain' make no diffunce who he talkin' wid, suh, he'd des stop right still en ax, 'Whar Trunion?' Den de niggers, dee got slack, en eve'y thing 'gun ter go een'-ways. One day I run up on Miss Lady settin' down cryin', en I ax her w'at de name er goodness de matter, en she say nuff de matter. Den I say she better go ask her pappy whar Trunion, en den she git red in de face, en 'low I better go 'ten' ter my business; en den I tell her dat ef somebody ain' tell us whar Trunion is, en dat mighty quick, dee won't be no business on dat place fer 'ten' ter. Yes, suh. I tol' her dat right p'intedly, suh.

"Well, suh, one day Marse Fess Trunion come a-drivin' up in a shiny double buggy, en he look like he des step right out'n a ban'-box; en ef ever I wuz glad ter see anybody, I wuz glad ter see dat man. Marster wuz glad; en dis time, suh, Miss Lady wuz glad, en she show it right plain; but Mistiss, she still sniff de a'r en hol' her head high. T'want long, suh, 'fo' we all knowd dat Marse Fess wuz gwine marry Miss Lady. I ain' know how dee fix it, kaze Mistiss never is come right out en say she 'greeable 'bout it, but Miss Lady wuz a Bledsoe too, en a Tomlinson ter boot, en I ain' never see nobody w'at impatient nuff fer ter stan' out 'g'inst dat gal. It ain' all happen, suh, quick ez I tell it, but it happen;

en but fer dat, I dunno w'at in de name er goodness
would er 'come er dis place."

A few hours later, as I sat with Trunion on the
veranda of his house, he verified Aunt Fountain's
story, but not until after he was convinced that I was
familiar with the history of the family. There was
much in that history he could afford to be proud of,
modern though he was. A man who believes in the
results of blood in cattle is not likely to ignore the
possibility of similar results in human beings; and I
think he regarded the matter in some such practical
light. He was a man, it seemed, who was disposed
to look lightly on trouble, once it was over with; and
I found he was not so much impressed with his
struggle against the positive scorn and contempt of
Mrs. Tomlinson, — a struggle that was infinitely more
important and protracted than Aunt Fountain had
described it to be, — as he was with his conflict with
Bermuda grass. He told me laughingly of some of
his troubles with his hot-headed neighbors in the
early days after the war, but nothing of this sort
seemed to be as important as his difficulties with
Bermuda grass. Here the practical and progressive
man showed himself; for I have a very vivid recollection of the desperate attempts of the farmers of
that region to uproot and destroy this particular
variety.

As for Trunion, he conquered it by cultivating it
for the benefit of himself and his neighbors; and I

suspect that this is the way he conquered his other opponents. It was a great victory over the grass, at any rate. I walked with him over the place, and the picture of it all is still framed in my mind, — the wonderful hedges of Cherokee roses, and the fragrant and fertile stretches of green Bermuda through which beautiful fawn-colored cattle were leisurely making their way. He had a theory that this was the only grass in the world fit for the dainty Jersey cow to eat.

There were comforts and conveniences on the Tomlinson Place not dreamed of in the old days, and I think there was substantial happiness there too. Trunion himself was a wholesome man, a man full of honest affection, hearty laughter, and hard work, — a breezy, companionable, energetic man. There was something boyish, unaffected, and winsome in his manners ; and I can easily understand why Judge Addison Tomlinson, in his old age, insisted on astonishing his family and his guests by exclaiming, "Where's Trunion ?" Certainly he was a man to think about and inquire after.

I have rarely seen a lovelier woman than his wife, and I think her happiness helped to make her so. She had inherited a certain degree of cold stateliness from her ancestors ; but her experience after the war, and Trunion's unaffected ways, had acted as powerful correctives, and there was nothing in the shape of indifference or haughtiness to mar her singular beauty.

As for Mrs. Tomlinson, — the habit is still strong
in me to call her Harriet Bledsoe, — I think that in
her secret soul she had an ineradicable contempt for
Trunion's extraordinary business energy. I think
his "push and vim," as the phrase goes, shocked
her sense of propriety to a far greater extent than
she would have been willing to admit. But she
had little time to think of these matters ; for she had
taken possession of her grandson, Master Addison
Tomlinson Trunion, and was absorbed in his wild
and boisterous ways, as grandmothers will be. This
boy, a brave and manly little fellow, had Trunion's
temper, but he had inherited the Tomlinson air. It
became him well, too, and I think Trunion was proud
of it.

"I am glad," said I, in parting, "that I have seen
Aunt Fountain's Prisoner."

"Ah !" said he, looking at his wife, who smiled
and blushed, "that was during the war. Since then
I have been a Prisoner of Peace."

I do not know what industrial theories Trunion
has impressed on his neighborhood by this time;
but he gave me a practical illustration of the fact
that one may be a Yankee and a Southerner too,
simply by being a large-hearted, whole-souled
American.

TROUBLE ON LOST MOUNTAIN.

THERE is no doubt that when Miss Babe Hightower stepped out on the porch, just after sun-
rise one fine morning in the spring of 1876, she had
the opportunity of enjoying a scene as beautiful as
any that nature offers to the human eye. She was
poised, so to speak, on the shoulder of Lost Mountain, a spot made cheerful and hospitable by her
father's industry, and by her own inspiring presence.
The scene, indeed, was almost portentous in its
beauty. Away above her the summit of the mountain was bathed in sunlight, while in the valley below
the shadows of dawn were still hovering, — a slow-
moving sea of transparent gray, touched here and
there with silvery reflections of light. Across the
face of the mountain that lifted itself to the skies, a
belated cloud trailed its wet skirts, revealing, as it
fled westward, a panorama of exquisite loveliness.
The fresh, tender foliage of the young pines, massed
here and there against the mountain side, moved and
swayed in the morning breeze until it seemed to be
a part of the atmosphere, a pale-green mist that
would presently mount into the upper air and melt
away. On a dead pine a quarter of a mile away, a

turkey-buzzard sat with wings outspread to catch the
warmth of the sun; while far above him, poised in
the illimitable blue, serene, almost motionless, as
though swung in the centre of space, his mate over-
looked the world.   The wild honeysuckles clambered
from bush to bush, and from tree to tree, mingling
their faint, sweet perfume with the delicious odors
that seemed to rise from the valley, and float down
from the mountain to meet in a little whirlpool of
fragrance in the porch where Miss Babe Hightower
stood.   The flowers and the trees could speak for
themselves; the slightest breeze gave them motion :
but the majesty of the mountain was voiceless; its
beauty was forever motionless.   Its silence seemed
more suggestive than the lapse of time, more profound than a prophet's vision of eternity, more
mysterious than any problem of the human mind.

It is fair to say, however, that Miss Babe Hightower did not survey the panorama that lay spread
out below her, around her, and above her, with any
peculiar emotions.   She was not without sentiment,
for she was a young girl just budding into womanhood, but all the scenery that the mountain or the
valley could show was as familiar to her as the fox-
hounds that lay curled up in the fence-corners, or
the fowls that crowed and clucked and cackled in the
yard.   She had discovered, indeed, that the individuality of the mountain was impressive, for she was
always lonely and melancholy when away from it;

but she viewed it, not as a picturesque affair to wonder at, but as a companion with whom she might hold communion. The mountain was something more than a mountain to her. Hundreds of times, when a little child, she had told it her small troubles, and it had seemed to her that the spirit of comfort dwelt somewhere near the precipitous summit. As she grew older the mountain played a less important part in her imagination, but she continued to regard it with a feeling of fellowship which she never troubled herself to explain or define.

Nevertheless, she did not step out on the porch to worship at the shrine of the mountain, or to enjoy the marvellous picture that nature presented to the eye. She went out in obedience to the shrilly uttered command of her mother, —

"Run, Babe, run! That pleggëd old cat's a-tryin' to drink out'n the water-bucket. Fling a cheer at 'er! Sick the dogs on 'er."

The cat, understanding the situation, promptly disappeared when it saw Babe, and the latter had nothing to do but make such demonstrations as are natural to youth, if not to beauty. She seized one of the many curious crystal formations which she had picked up on the mountain, and employed for various purposes of ornamentation, and sent it flying after the cat. She threw with great strength and accuracy, but the cat was gone. The crystal went zooning into the fence-corner where one of the hounds lay; and this sensitive creature, taking it for granted that he had been made the special object of attack, set up a series of loud yells by way of protest. This aroused the rest of the dogs, and in a moment that particular part of the mountain was in an uproar. Just at that instant a stalwart man came around the corner of the house. He was bareheaded, and wore neither coat nor vest. He was tall and well made, though rather too massive to be supple. His beard, which was full and flowing, was plentifully streaked with gray. His appearance would have been strikingly ferocious but for his eyes, which showed a nature at once simple and humorous, — and certainly the strongly moulded, square-set jaws, and the firm lips needed some such pleasant corrective.

"Great Jerusalem, Babe!" cried this mild-eyed giant. "What could 'a' possessed you to be a-chunkin' ole Blue that away? Ag'in bullaces is ripe you'll git your heart sot on 'possum, an' whar' is the 'possum comin' from ef ole Blue's laid up? Blame my hide ef you ain't a-cuttin' up some mighty quare capers fer a young gal."

"Why, Pap!" exclaimed Babe, as soon as she could control her laughter, "that rock didn't tetch ole Blue. He's sech a make-believe, I'm a great mind to hit him a clip jest to show you how he can go on."

"Now, don't do that, honey," said her father. "Ef

you want to chunk anybody, chunk me. I kin holler lots purtier'n ole Blue. An' ef you don't want to chunk me chunk your mammy fer ole acquaintance sake. She's big an' fat."

"Oh, Lordy!" exclaimed Mrs. Hightower from the inside of the house. "Don't set her atter me, Abe, — don't, fer mercy's sake. Get her in the notion, an' she'll be a-yerkin' me aroun' thereckly like I wuz a rag-baby. I'm a-gittin' too ole fer ter be romped aroun' by a great big double-j'inted gal like Babe. Projick wi' 'er yourself, but make 'er let me alone."

Abe turned and went around the house again, leaving his daughter standing on the porch, her cheeks glowing, and her black eyes sparkling with laughter. Babe loitered on the porch a moment, looking into the valley. The gray mists had lifted themselves into the upper air, and the atmosphere was so clear that the road leading to the mountain could be followed by the eye, save where it ran under the masses of foliage; and it seemed to be a most devious and versatile road, turning back on itself at one moment only to plunge boldly forward the next. Nor was it lacking in color. On the levels it was of dazzling whiteness, shining like a pool of water; but at points where it made a visible descent, it was alternately red and gray. Something or other on this variegated road attracted Miss Babe's attention, for she shaded her eyes with her hand, and leaned forward. Presently she cried out, —

" Pap!—oh, pap! there's a man a-ridin' up Peevy's Ridge."

This information was repeated by Babe's mother ; and in a few moments the porch, which was none too commodious, though it was very substantial, was occupied by the entire Hightower family, which in-cluded Grandsir Hightower, a white-haired old man, whose serenity seemed to be borrowed from another world. Mrs. Hightower herself was a stout, motherly-looking woman, whose whole appearance betokened contentment, if not happiness. Abe shaded his eyes with his broad hand, and looked towards Peevy's Ridge.

" I reckon maybe it's Tuck Peevy hisse'f," Mrs. Hightower remarked.

" That's who I 'lowed hit wuz," said Grandsir Hightower, in the tone of one who had previously made up his mind.

" Well, I reckon I ought to know Tuck Peevy," exclaimed Babe.

" That's so," said Grandsir Hightower. " Babe oughter know Tuck. She oughter know him certain an' shore ; bekaze he's bin a-floppin' in an' out er this house ever' Sunday fer mighty nigh two year'. Some sez he likes Babe, an' some sez he likes Susan's fried chicken. Now, in my day and time " —

" He's in the dreen now," said Babe, interrupting her loquacious grandparent, who threatened to make some embarrassing remark. " He's a-ridin' a gray."

"He's a mighty early bird," said Abe, "less'n he's a-headin' fer the furder side. Maybe he's a revenue man," he continued. "They say they're a-gwine to heat the hills mighty hot from this on."

"You hain't got nothing gwine on down on the branch, is you, Abe?" inquired Grandsir Hightower, with pardonable solicitude.

"Well," said Abe evasively, "I hain't kindled no fires yit, but you better b'lieve I'm a-gwine to keep my beer from sp'ilin'. The way I do my countin', one tub of beer is natchally wuth two revenue chaps."

By this time the horseman who had attracted Babe's attention came into view again. Abe studied him a moment, and remarked, —

"That hoss steps right along, an' the chap a-straddle of him is got on store-clo'es. Fetch me my rifle, Babe. I'll meet that feller half-way an' make some inquirements about his famerly, an' maybe I'll fetch a squir'l back."

With this Abe called to his dogs, and started off.

"Better keep your eye open, Pap," cried Sis. "Maybe it's the sheriff."

Abe paused a moment, and then pretended to be hunting a stone with which to demolish his daughter, whereupon Babe ran laughing into the house. The allusion to the sheriff was a stock joke in the Hightower household, though none of them made such free use of it as Babe, who was something more than

a privileged character, so far as her father was concerned. On one occasion shortly after the war, Abe
had gone to the little county town on business, and
had been vexed into laying rough hands on one of
the prominent citizens who was a trifle under the
influence of liquor. A warrant was issued, and Dave
McLendon, the sheriff of the county, a stumpy little
man, whose boldness and prudence made him the
terror of criminals, was sent to serve it. Abe, who
was on the lookout for some such visitation, saw him
coming, and prepared himself. He stood in the
doorway, with his rifle flung carelessly across his left
arm.

"Hold on thar, Dave!" he cried, as the latter
came up. The sheriff, knowing his man, halted.

"I hate to fling away my manners, Dave," he went
on, "but folks is gittin' to be mighty funny these
days. A man's obleeged to s'arch his best frien's
'fore he kin find out the'r which-aways. Dave, what
sort of a dockyment is you got ag'in' me?"

"I got a warrant, Abe," said the sheriff pleasantly.

"Well, Dave, hit won't fetch me," said Abe.

"Oh, yes!" said the sheriff. "Yes, it will, Abe.
I bin a-usin' these kind er warrants a mighty long
time, an' they fetches a feller every whack."

"Now, I'll tell you what, Dave," said Abe, patting
his rifle, "I got a dockyment here that'll fetch you a
blame sight quicker'n your dockyment'll fetch me;

an' I tell you right now, plain an' flat, I hain't a-gwine to be drug aroun' an' slapped in jail."

The sheriff leaned carelessly against the rail fence in the attitude of a man who is willing to argue an interesting question.

"Well, I tell you how I feel about it, Abe," said the sheriff, speaking very slowly. "You kin shoot me, but you can't shoot the law. Bang away at me, an' thar's another warrant atter you. This yer one what I'm already got don't amount to shucks, so you better fling on your coat, saddle your horse, an' go right along wi' me thes ez neighborly ez you please."

"Dave," said Abe, "if you come in at that gate you er a goner."

"Well, Abe," the sheriff replied, "I 'lowed you'd kick; I know what human natur' on these hills is, an' so I thes axed some er the boys to come along. They er right down thar in the holler. They hain't got no mo' idea what I come fer'n the man in the moon; yit they'd make a mighty peart posse. Tooby shore, a great big man like you ain't afeard fer ter face a little bit er law."

Abe Hightower hesitated a moment, and then went into the house. In a few minutes he issued forth and went out to the gate where the sheriff was. The faces of the two men were a study. Neither betrayed any emotion nor alluded to the warrant. The sheriff asked after the "crap;" and Abe told him it was "middlin' peart," and asked him to go

into the house and make himself at home until the
horse could be saddled. After a while the two rode
away. Once during the ride Abe said, —

"I'm mighty glad it wa'n't that feller what run
ag'in' you last fall, Dave."

"Why?" asked the sheriff.

"Bekaze I'd 'a' plugged him, certain an' shore,"
said Abe.

"Well," said the sheriff, laughing, "I wuz a-wish-
in' mighty hard thes about that time that the t'other
feller had got 'lected."

The warrant amounted to nothing, and Abe was
soon at home with his family; but it suited his high-
spirited daughter to twit him occasionally because of
his tame surrender to the sheriff, and it suited Dave
to treat the matter good-humoredly.

Abe Hightower took his way down the mountain;
and about two miles from his house, as the road ran,
he met the stranger who had attracted Babe's attention. He was a handsome young fellow, and he was
riding a handsome horse, — a gray, that was evidently
used to sleeping in a stable where there was plenty
of feed in the trough. The rider also had a well-fed
appearance. He sat his horse somewhat jauntily,
and there was a jocund expression in his features
very pleasing to behold. He drew rein as he saw
Abe, and gave a military salute in a careless, off-hand
way that was in strict keeping with his appearance.

"Good-morning, sir," he said.

"Howdy?" said Abe.

"Fine day this."

"Well, what little I've saw of it is purty tollerbul."

The young fellow laughed, and his laughter was worth hearing. It had the ring of youth in it.

"Do you chance to know a Mr. Hightower?" he asked, throwing a leg over the pommel of the saddle.

"Do he live anywheres aroun' in these parts?" Abe inquired.

"So I'm told."

"Well, the reason I ast," said Abe, leaning his rifle against a tree, "is bekaze they mought be more'n one Hightower runnin' loose."

"You don't know him, then?"

"I know one on 'em. Any business wi' him?"

"Well, yes, — a little. I was told he lived on this road. How far is his house?"

"Well, I'll tell you," — Abe took off his hat and scratched his head, — "some folks mought take a notion hit wuz a long ways off, an' then, ag'in, yuther folks mought take a notion that hit wuz lots nigher. Hit's accordin' to the way you look at it."

"Is Mr. Hightower at home?" inquired the young stranger, regarding Abe with some degree of curiosity.

"Well," said Abe cautiously, "I don't reckon he's right slam bang at home, but I lay he ain't fur off."

"If you happen to see him, pray tell him there's

a gentleman at his house who would like very much
to see him."

"Well, I tell you what, mister," said Abe, speaking
very slowly. "You're a mighty nice young feller, —
anybody kin shet the'r eyes and see that, — but folks
'roun' here is mighty kuse; they is that away. Ef I
was you, I'd thes turn right 'roun' in my tracks 'n' let
that ar Mister Hightower alone. I wouldn't pester
wi' 'im. He hain't no fitten company fer you."

"Oh, but I must see him," said the stranger. "I
have business with him. Why, they told me down
in the valley that Hightower, in many respects, is
the best man in the county."

Abe smiled for the first time. It was the ghost of
a smile.

"Shoo!" he exclaimed. "They don't know him
down thar nigh as good as he's know'd up here. An'
that hain't all. Thish yer Mister Hightower you er
talkin' about is got a mighty bad case of measles at
his house. You'd be ableedze to ketch 'em ef you
went thar."

"I've had the measles," said the stranger.

"But these here measles," persisted Abe, half
shutting his eyes and gazing at the young man steadily, "kin be cotched twice-t. Theyer wuss 'n the
small-pox, — lots wuss."

"My dear sir, what do you mean?" the young man
inquired, observing the significant emphasis of the
mountaineer's language.

"Hit's thes like I tell you," said Abe. "Looks like folks has mighty bad luck when they go a-rippit-in' hether an' yan on the mounting. It hain't been sech a monst'us long time sence one er them rev-nue fellers come a-paradin' up thish yer same road, a-makin' inquirements for Hightower. *He* cotch the measles; bless you, he took an' cotch 'em by the time he got in hailin' distance of Hightower's, an' he had to be toted down. I disremember his name, but he wuz a mighty nice-lookin' young feller, peart an' soople, an' thes about your size an' weight."

"It was no doubt a great pity about the revenue chap," said the young man sarcastically.

"Lor', yes!" exclaimed Abe seriously; "lots er nice folks must 'a' cried about that man."

"Well," said the other smiling, "I must see High-tower. I guess he's a nicer man than his neighbors think he is."

"Shoo!" said Abe, "he hain't a bit nicer'n what I am, an' I lay he hain't no purtier. What mought be your name, mister?"

"My name is Chichester, and I'm buying land for some Boston people. I want to buy some land right on this mountain if I can get it cheap enough."

"Jesso," said Abe, "but wharbouts in thar do Hightower come in?"

"Oh, he knows all about the mountain, and I want to ask his advice and get his opinions," said Chichester.

Something about Mr. Chichester seemed to attract Abe Hightower. Perhaps it was the young fellow's fresh, handsome appearance; perhaps it was his free-and-easy attitude, suggestive of the commercial tourist, that met the approbation of the mountaineer. At any rate, Abe smiled upon the young man in a fatherly way and said, —

"'Twixt you an' me an' yon pine, you hain't got no furder to go fer to strike up wi' Hightower. I'm the man you er atter."

Chichester regarded him with some degree of amazement.

"My dear sir," he exclaimed, "why should you desire to play the sphinx?"

"Spinks?" said Abe, with something like a grimace; "the Spinks famerly lived furder up the mounting, but they er done bin weeded out by the revenue men too long ago to talk about. The ole man's in jail in Atlanty er some'rs else, the boys is done run'd off, an' the gal's a trollop. No Spinks in mine, cap', *ef* you please!"

Chichester laughed at the other's earnestness. He mistook it for drollery.

"I let you know, cap'," Abe went on, "you can't be boss er your own doin's an' give ever' passin' man your name."

"Well, I'm very glad to meet you," said Chichester heartily; "I'll have a good deal of business in this neighborhood first and last, and I'm told there isn't any thing worth knowing about the mountain that you don't know."

"That kind er talk," Abe replied, "kin be run in the groun', yit I hain't a-denyin' but what I've got a kind er speakin' acquaintance wi' the neighborhood whar I'm a-livin' at. Ef you er huntin' my house, thes drive right on. I'll be thar ag'in you git thar."

Chichester found a very cordial welcome awaiting him when he arrived at Hightower's house. Even the dogs were friendly, and the big cat came out from its hiding-place to rub against his legs as he sat on the little porch.

"By the time you rest your face an' han's," said Abe, "I reckon breakfast'll be ready."

Chichester, who was anxious to give no trouble, explained that he had had a cup of coffee at Peevy's before starting up the mountain. He said, moreover, that the mountain was so bracing that he felt as if he could fast a week and still fatten.

"Well, sir," Abe remarked, "hit's mighty little we er got to offer, an' that little's mighty common, but, sech as 'tis, you er more'n welcome. Hit's diffunt wi' me when the mornin' air blows at me. Hit makes me wanter nibble at somepin'. I dunner whar you come from, an' I ain't makin' no inquirements, but down in these parts you can't spat a man harder betwixt the eyes than to set back an' not break bread wi' 'im."

Mr. Chichester had been warned not to wound the hospitality of the simple people among whom he was going, and he was quick to perceive that his refusal to "break bread" with the Hightowers would be taken too seriously. Whereupon, he made a most substantial apology, — an apology that took the shape of a ravenous appetite, and did more than justice to Mrs. Hightower's fried chicken, crisp biscuits, and genuine coffee. Mr. Chichester also made himself as agreeable as he knew how, and he was so pleased with the impression he made that he, on his side, admitted to himself that the Hightowers were charmingly quaint, especially the shy girl of whom he caught a brief glimpse now and then as she handed her mother fresh supplies of chicken and biscuits.

There was nothing mysterious connected with the visit of Mr. Chichester to Lost Mountain. He was the agent of a company of Boston capitalists who were anxious to invest money in Georgia marble-quarries, and Chichester was on Lost Mountain for the purpose of discovering the marble beds that had been said by some to exist there. He had the versatility of a modern young man, being something of a civil engineer and something of a geologist; in fine, he was one of the many "general-utility" men that improved methods enable the high schools and colleges to turn out. He was in the habit of making himself agreeable wherever he went, but behind his levity and general good humor there was a good deal of seriousness and firmness of purpose.

He talked with great freedom to the Hightowers, giving a sort of commercial coloring, so to speak, to the plans of his company with respect to land investments on Lost Mountain; but he said nothing about his quest for marble.

"The Lord send they won't be atter fetchin' the railroad kyars among us," said Grandsir Hightower fervently.

"Well, sir," said Chichester, "there isn't much danger."

"Now, I dunno 'bout that," said the old man querulously, "I dunno 'bout that. They're gittin' so these days they'll whirl in an' do e'enamost any thing what you don't want 'em to do. I kin stan' out thar in the hoss-lot any cle'r day an' see the smoke er their ingines, an' sometimes hit looks like I kin hear 'em snort an' cough. They er plenty nigh enough. The Lord send they won't fetch 'em no nigher. Fum Giner'l Jackson's time plump tell now, they er bin a-fetchin' destruction to the country. You'll see it. I mayn't see it myself, but you'll see it. Fust hit was Giner'l Jackson an' the bank, an' now hit's the railroad kyars. You'll see it!"

"And yet," said Chichester, turning towards the old man, as Hope might beam benignantly on the Past, "everybody and every thing seems to be getting along very well. I think the only thing necessary now is to invent something or other to keep the cinders out of a man's eyes when he rides on the railroads."

"Don't let 'em fool you," said the old man earnestly. "Ever' thing's in a tangle, an' ther hain't no Whig party for to ontangle it. Giner'l Jackson an' the cussid bank is what done it."

Just then Miss Babe came out on the little porch, and seated herself on the bench that ran across one end. "Cap'," said Abe, with some show of embarrassment, as if not knowing how to get through a necessary ceremony, "this is my gal, Babe. She's the oldest and the youngest. I'm name' Abe an' she's name' Babe, sort er rhymin' like."

The unaffected shyness of the young girl was pleasant to behold, and if it did not heighten her beauty, it certainly did not detract from it. It was a shyness in which there was not an awkward element, for Babe had the grace of youth and beauty, and conscious independence animated all her movements.

"'Ceppin' me an' the ole 'oman," said Abe, "Babe is the best-lookin' one er the famerly."

The girl reddened a little, and laughed lightly with the air of one who is accustomed to give and take jokes, but said nothing.

"I heard of Miss Babe last night," said Chichester, "and I've got a message for her."

"Wait!" exclaimed Abe triumphantly; "I'll bet a hoss I kin call the name 'thout movin' out'n my cheer. Hold on!" he continued. "I'll bet another hoss I kin relate the message word for word."

Babe blushed violently, but laughed good-humoredly. Chichester adjusted himself at once to this unexpected informality, and allowed himself to become involved in it.

"Come, now!" he exclaimed, "I'll take the bet."

"I declare!" said Mrs. Hightower, laughing, "you all oughtn' to pester Babe that away."

"Wait!" said Abe. "The name er the man what sont the word is Tuck Peevy, an' when he know'd you was a-comin' here, he sort er sidled up an' ast you for to please be so good as to tell Miss Babe he'd drap in nex' Sunday, an' see what her mammy is a-gwine ter have for dinner."

"Well, I have won the bet," said Chichester. "Mr. Peevy simply asked me to tell Miss Babe that there would be a singing at Philadelphia camp-ground Sunday. I hardly know what to do with two horses."

"Maybe you'll feel better," said Abe, "when somebody tells you that my hoss is a mule. Well, well, well!" he went on. "Tuck didn't say he was comin', but I be boun' he comes, an' more'n that, I be boun' a whole passel er gals an' boys'll foller Babe home."

"In giner'lly," said Grandsir Hightower, "I hate

for to make remarks 'bout folks when they hain't
settin' whar they kin hear me, but that ar Tuck
Peevy is got a mighty bad eye.   I hearn 'im a-quollin'
wi' one er them Simmons boys las' Sunday gone
wuz a week, an' I tell you he's got the Ole Boy in
'im.   An' his appetite's wuss'n his eye."

"Well," said Mrs. Hightower, "nobody 'roun'
here don't begrudge him his vittles, I reckon."

"Oh, by no means, — by no manner er means,"
said the old man, suddenly remembering the presence of Chichester.   "Yit they oughter be reason
in all things; that's what I say, — reason in all
things, speshually when hit comes to gormandizin'."

The evident seriousness of the old man was very
comical.   He seemed to be possessed by the unrea-
sonable economy that not infrequently seizes on old
age.

"They hain't no begrudgin' 'roun' here," he went
on.   "Lord! ef I'd 'a' bin a-begrudgin' I'd 'a' thes
natchally bin e't up wi' my begrudges.   What wer'
the word the poor creetur sent to Babe?"

Chichester repeated the brief and apparently
uninteresting message, and Grandsir Hightower
groaned dismally.

"I dunner what sot him so ag'in Tuck Peevy,"
said Abe, laughing.   "Tuck's e'en about the peart-
est chap in the settlement, an' a mighty handy man,
put him whar you will."

"Why, Aberham!" exclaimed the old man, "you

go on like a man what's done gone an' took leave of his sev'm senses. You dunner what sot me ag'in' the poor creetur? Why, time an' time ag'in I've tol' you it's his ongodly hankerin' atter the flesh-pots. The Bible's ag'in' it, an' I'm ag'in it. Whar-bouts is it put down that a man is ever foun' grace in the cubberd?"

"Well, I lay a man that works is boun' ter eat," said Abe.

"Oh, *I* hain't no 'count, — *I* can't work," said the old man, his wrath, which had been wrought to a high pitch, suddenly taking the shape of plaintive humility. "Yit 'tain't for long. *I'll* soon be out'n the way, Aberham."

"Shoo!" said Abe, placing his hand affectionately on the old man's shoulder. "You er mighty nigh as spry as a kitten. Babe, honey, fill your grandsir's pipe. He's a-missin' his mornin' smoke."

Soothed by his pipe, the old man seemed to forget the existence of Tuck Peevy, and his name came up for discussion no more.

But Chichester, being a man of quick perceptions, gathered from the animosity of the old man, and the rather uneasy attitude of Miss Babe, that the discussion of Peevy's appetite had its origin in the lover-like attentions which he had been paying to the girl. Certainly Peevy was excusable, and if his attentions had been favorably received, he was to be congratulated, Chichester thought; for in all that region it would have been difficult to find a lovelier specimen of budding womanhood than the young girl who had striven so unsuccessfully to hide her embarrassment as her grandfather proceeded, with the merciless recklessness of age, to criticise Peevy's strength and weakness as a trencherman.

As Chichester had occasion to discover afterwards, Peevy had his peculiarities; but he did not seem to be greatly different from other young men to be found in that region. One of his peculiarities was that he never argued about any thing. He had opinions on a great many subjects, but his reasons for holding his opinions he kept to himself. The arguments of those who held contrary views he would listen to with great patience, even with interest; but his only reply would be a slow, irritating smile and a shake of the head. Peevy was homely, but there was nothing repulsive about his homeliness. He was tall and somewhat angular; he was sallow; he had high cheek-bones, and small eyes that seemed to be as alert and as watchful as those of a ferret; and he was slow and deliberate in all his movements, taking time to digest and consider his thoughts before replying to the simplest question, and even then his reply was apt to be evasive. But he was good-humored and obliging, and, consequently, was well thought of by his neighbors and acquaintances.

There was one subject in regard to which he made

no concealment, and that was his admiration for Miss Babe Hightower. So far as Peevy was concerned, she was the one woman in the world. His love for her was a passion at once patient, hopeful, and innocent. He displayed his devotion less in words than in his attitude ; and so successful had he been that it was generally understood that by camp-meeting time Miss Babe' Hightower would be Mrs. Tuck Peevy. That is to say, it was understood by all except Grandsir Hightower, who was apt to chuckle sarcastically when the subject was broached.

"They hain't arry livin' man," he would say, "what's ever seed anybody wi' them kind er eyes settled down an' married. No, sirs! Hit's the vittles Tuck Peevy's atter. Why, bless your soul an' body! he thes natchally dribbles at the mouth when he gits a whiff from the dinner-pot."

Certainly no one would have supposed that Tuck Peevy ever had a sentimental emotion or a romantic notion, but Grandsir Hightower did him great injustice. Behind his careless serenity he was exceedingly sensitive. It is true he was a man difficult to. arouse ; but he was what his friends called "a mighty tetchy man" on some subjects, and one of these subjects was Babe. Another was the revenue men. It was generally supposed by Peevy's acquaintances on Lost Mountain, that he had a moonshine apparatus over on Sweetwater ; but this supposition was the result, doubtless, of his well-known preju dice against the deputies sent out to enforce the revenue laws.

It had been the intention of Chichester to remain only a few days in that neighborhood ; but the Hightowers were so hospitably inclined, and the outcroppings of minerals so interesting, that his stay was somewhat prolonged. Naturally, he saw a good deal of Peevy, who knew all about the mountain, and who was frequently able to go with him on his little excursions when Abe Hightower was otherwise engaged. Naturally enough, too, Chichester saw a great deal of Babe. He was interested in her because she was young and beautiful, and because of her quaint individuality. She was not only unconventional, but charmingly so. Her crudeness and her ignorance seemed to be merely phases of originality.

Chichester's interest in Babe was that of a studiously courteous and deferent observer, but it was jealously noted and resented by Tuck Peevy. The result of this was not at first apparent. For a time Peevy kept his jealous suggestions to himself, but he found it impossible to conceal their effect. Gradually, he held himself aloof, and finally made it a point to avoid Chichester altogether. For a time Babe made the most of her lover's jealousy. After the manner of her sex, she was secretly delighted to discover that he was furious at the thought that she might inadvertently have cast a little bit of a smile

at Mr. Chichester; and on several occasions she
heartily enjoyed Peevy's angry suspicions. But after
a while she grew tired of such inconsistent and foolish manifestations. They made her unhappy, and
she was too vigorous and too practical to submit to
unhappiness with that degree of humility which her
more cultivated sisters sometimes exhibit.

One Sunday afternoon, knowing Chichester to be
away, Tuck Peevy sauntered carelessly into Hightower's yard, and seated himself on the steps of the
little porch. It was his first visit for several days,
and Babe received him with an air of subdued coolness and indifference that did credit to her sex.

"Wharbouts is your fine gent this mornin'?"
inquired Peevy, after a while.

"Wharbouts is who?"

"Your fine gent wi' the sto'-clo'es on."

"I reckon you mean Cap'n Chichester, don't you?"
inquired Babe innocently.

"Oh, yes!" exclaimed Peevy; "he's the chap I'm
a-making my inquirements atter."

"He's over on Sweetwater, I reckon. Leastways
thar's whar he started to go,"

"On Sweetwater. Oh, yes!" Peevy paused and
ran his long slim fingers through his thin straight
hair. "I'm mighty much afeard," he went on after
a pause, "that that fine gent o' yourn is a-gwine ter
turn out for to be a snake. That's what I'm afeard
un."

"Well," said Babe, with irritating coolness, "he don't do any of his sneakin' aroun' here. Ef he sneaks, he goes some'ers else to sneak. He don't hang aroun' an' watch his chance to drap in an' pay his calls. I reckon he'd walk right in at the gate thar ef he know'd the Gov'ner er the State wuz a-settin' here. I'm mighty glad I hain't saw none er his sneakin'."

Peevy writhed under this comment on his own actions, but said nothing in reply.

"You don't come to see folks like you useter," said Babe, softening a little. "I reckon you er mighty busy down thar wi' your craps."

Peevy smiled until he showed his yellow teeth. It was not intended to be a pleasant smile.

"I reckon I come lots more'n I'm wanted," he replied. "I hain't got much sense," he went on, "but I got a leetle bit, an' I know when my room's wuth more'n my comp'ny."

"Your hints has got more wings'n stings," said Babe. "But ef I had in my min' what you er got in yourn" —

"Don't say the word, Babe!" exclaimed Peevy, for the first time fixing his restless eyes on her face. "Don't!"

"Yes, I'll say it," said Babe solemnly. "I oughter 'a' said it a long time ago when you wuz a-cuttin' up your capers bekaze Phli Varnadoe wuz a-comin' here to see Pap. I oughter 'a' said it then, but I'll say it

now, right pine-blank. Ef I had in my min' what
you er got in yourn, I wouldn't never darken this
door no more."

Peevy rose, and walked up and down the porch.
He was deeply moved, but his face showed his emotion only by a slight increase of sallowness. Finally
he paused, and looked at Babe.

"I lay you'd be mighty glad ef I didn't come no
more," he said, with a half smile. "I reckon it
kinder rankles you for to see old Tuck Peevy a-hangin' roun' when the t'other feller's in sight."

Babe's only reply was a scornful toss of the head.

"Oh, yes!" Peevy went on, "hit rankles you
might'ly; yit I lay it won't rankle you so much atter
your daddy is took an' jerked off to Atlanty. I tell
you, Babe, that ar man is one er the revenues — they
hain't no two ways about that."

Babe regarded her angry lover seriously.

" Hit ain't no wonder you make up your min' ag'in'
him when you er done made it up ag'in' me. I know
in reason they must be somep'n 'nother wrong when
a great big grown man kin work hisself up to holdin'
spite. Goodness knows, I wish you wuz like you
useter be when I fust know'd you."

Peevy's sallow face flushed a little at the re-
membrance of those pleasant, peaceful days; but,
somehow, the memory of them had the effect of in-
tensifying his jealous mood.

" 'Tain't me that's changed aroun'," he exclaimed

passionately, "an' 'tain't the days nuther. Hit's you, — you! An' that fine gent that's a-hanging roun' here is the 'casion of it. Ever'whar I go, hit's the talk. Babe, you know you er lovin' that man!"

Peevy was wide of the mark, but the accusation was so suddenly and so bluntly made that it brought the blood to Babe's face, — a tremulous flush that made her fairly radiant for a moment. Undoubtedly Mr. Chichester had played a very pleasing part in her youthful imagination, but never for an instant had he superseded the homely figure of Tuck Peevy. The knowledge that she was blushing gave Babe an excuse for indignation that women are quick to take advantage of. She was so angry, indeed, that she made another mistake.

"Why, Tuck Peevy!" she cried, "you shorely must be crazy. He wouldn't wipe his feet on sech as me!"

"No," said Peevy, "I 'lowed he wouldn't, an' I 'lowed as how you wouldn't wipe your feet on me." He paused a moment, still smiling his peculiar smile. "Hit's a long ways down to Peevy, ain't it?"

"You er doin' all the belittlin'," said Babe.

"Oh, no, Babe! Ever'thing's changed. Why, even them dogs barks atter me. Ever'thing's turned wrong-sud-outerds. An' you er changed wuss'n all."

"Well, you don't reckon I'm a-gwine ter run out'n the gate thar an' fling myself at you, do you?" exclaimed Babe.

"No, I don't. I've thes come to-day for to git a cle'r understan'in'." He hesitated a moment and then went on : "Babe, will you marry me to-morrow ? " He asked the question with more eagerness than he had yet displayed.

"No, I won't!" exclaimed Babe, "ner the nex' day nuther. The man I marry'll have a lots better opinion of me than what you er got."

Babe was very indignant, but she paused to see what effect her words would have. Peevy rubbed his hands nervously together, but he made no response. His serenity was more puzzling than that of the mountain. He still smiled vaguely, but it was not a pleasing smile. He looked hard at Babe for a moment, and then down at his clumsy feet. His agitation was manifest, but it did not take the shape of words. In the trees overhead two jays were quarrelling with a cat-bird, and in the upper air a bee-martin was fiercely pursuing a sparrow-hawk.

"Well," he said, after a while, "I reckon I better be gwine."

"Wait till your hurry's over," said Babe, in a gentler tone.

Peevy made no reply, but passed out into the road, and disappeared down the mountain. Babe followed him to the gate, and stood looking after him ; but he turned his head neither to the right nor to the left, and in a little while she went into the house with her head bent upon her bosom. She was weeping.

Grandsir Hightower, who had shuffled out on the porch to sun himself, stared at the girl with amazement.

"Why, honey!" he exclaimed, "what upon the top side er the yeth ails you?"

"Tuck has gone home mad, an' he won't never come back no more," she cried.

"What's the matter wi' 'im?"

"Oh, he's thes mad along er me."

"Well, well, well!" exclaimed the old man, fumbling feebly in his pockets for his red bandanna handkerchief, "what kind of a come-off is this? Did you ast him to stay to dinner, honey?"

"No — no; he didn't gimme a chance."

"I 'lowed you didn't," exclaimed Grandsir Hightower triumphantly. "I thes natchally 'lowed you didn't. That's what riled 'im. An' now he'll go off an' vilify you. Well, well, well! he's missed his dinner! The fust time in many's the long day. Watch 'im, Babe! Watch 'im, honey! The Ole Boy's in 'im. I know 'im; I've kep' my two eyes on 'im. For a mess er turnip-greens an' dumperlin's that man 'u'd do murder." The old man paused and looked all around, as if by that means to dissipate a suspicion that he was dreaming. "An' so Tuck missed his dinner! Tooby shore, — tooby shore!"

"Oh, hit ain't that," cried Babe; "he's jealous of Cap'n Chichester."

"Why, the good Lord, honey! what makes you run on that away?"

"He tol' me so," said Babe.

"Jealous!" exclaimed Grandsir Hightower, "jealous er that young feller! Merciful powers, honey! he's a-begrudgin' 'im the vittles what he eats. I know'd it the minnit I seed 'im come a-sa'nterin' in the yard. Lord, Lord! I wish in my soul the poor creetur could git a chance at one er them ar big Whig barbecues what they useter have."

But there was small consolation in all this for Babe; and she went into the house, where her forlorn appearance attracted the attention of her mother.

"Why, Babe! what in the worl'!" exclaimed this practical woman, dropping her work in amazement. "What in the name er sense ails you?"

Babe had no hesitation in telling her mother the facts.

"Well, my goodness!" was Mrs. Hightower's comment, "I wouldn't go aroun' whinin' about it, ef I wuz you—that I wouldn't. Nobody never ketched me whinin' 'roun' atter your pappy 'fore we wuz married, an' he wuz lots purtier than what Tuck Peevy is. When your pappy got tetchy, I thes says to myself, s'I, 'Ef I'm wuth havin', I'm wuth scramblin' atter;' an' ef your pappy hadn't 'a' scrambled an' scuffled 'roun' he wouldn't 'a' got me nuther, ef I do up an' say it myself. I'd a heap druther see you fillin' them slays an' a-fixin' up for to weave your pappy some

shirts, than to see you a-whinin' 'roun' atter any chap
on the top side er the yeth, let 'lone Tuck Peevy.''

There was little consolation even in this, but Babe
went about her simple duties with some show of
spirit ; and when her father and Chichester returned
from their trip on Sweetwater, it would have required a sharp eye to discover that Babe regarded
herself as "wearing the green willow."

For a few days she avoided Chichester, as if by
that means to prove her loyalty to Peevy ; but as
Peevy was not present to approve her conduct or to
take advantage of it, she soon grew tired of playing
an unnecessary part. Peevy persisted in staying
away ; and the result was, that Babe's anger — a
healthy quality in a young girl — got the better of her
grief. Then wonder took the place of anger ; but
behind it all was the hope that before many days
Peevy would saunter into the house, armed with his
inscrutable smile, and inquire, as he had done a hundred times before, how long before dinner would be
ready. This theory was held by Grandsir Hightower,
but, as it was a very plausible one, Babe adopted it
as her own.

Meanwhile, it is not to be supposed that two
lovers, one sulking and the other sighing, had any
influence on the season. The spring had made some
delay in the valley before taking complete possession
of the mountain, but this delay was not significant.
Even on the mountain, the days began to suggest

the ardor of summer. The air was alternately warm and hazy, and crisp and clear. One day Kenesaw would cast aside its atmospheric trappings, and appear to lie within speaking distance of Hightower's door ; the next, it would withdraw behind its blue veil, and seem far enough away to belong to another world. On Hightower's farm the corn was high enough to whet its green sabres against the wind.

One evening Chichester, Hightower, and Babe sat on the little porch with their faces turned toward Kenesaw. They had been watching a line of blue smoke on the mountain in the distance ; and, as the twilight deepened into dusk, they saw that the summit of Kenesaw was crowned by a thin fringe of fire. As the darkness gathered, the bright belt of flame projected against the vast expanse of night seemed to belong to the vision of St. John.

"It looks like a picture out of the Bible," suggested Chichester somewhat vaguely.

"It's wuss'n that, I reckon," said Abe. "Some un's a-losin' a mighty sight of fencin' ; an' timber's timber these days, lemme tell you."

"Maybe some un's a-burnin' bresh," said Babe.

"Bless you ! they don't pile bresh in a streak a mile long," said Abe.

The thin line of fire crept along slowly, and the people on the little porch sat and watched it. Occasionally it would crawl up to the top of a dead pine, and leave a fiery signal flaming in the air.

"What is the matter with Peevy?" asked Chichester after a while. "I met him on the mountain the
other day, and he seemed not to know me."

"He don't know anybody aroun' here," said Babe
with a sigh.

"Hit's thes some er his an' Babe's capers,"
Hightower remarked with a laugh. "They er bin
a-cuttin' up this away now gwine on two year'. I
reckon ag'in' camp-meetin' time Tuck'll drap in an'
make hisself know'd. Gals and boys is mighty
funny wi' the'r gwines-on."

After a little, Abe went into the house, and left
the young people to watch the fiery procession on
Kenesaw.

"The next time I see Peevy," said Chichester
gallantly, "I'll take him by the sleeve, and show him
the road to Beauty's bower."

"Well, you nee'nter pester wi' 'im on account of
me," said Babe. Chichester laughed. The fact that
so handsome a girl as Babe should deliberately fall
in love with so lank and ungainly a person as Tuck
Peevy, seemed to him to be one of the problems
that philosophers ought to concern themselves with;
but, from his point of view, the fact that Babe had
not gradually faded away, according to the approved
rules of romance, was entirely creditable to human
nature on the mountain.

A candle, burning in the room that Chichester
occupied, shone through the window faintly, and fell

on Babe, while Chichester sat in the shadow. As they were talking, a mocking-bird in the apple-trees awoke, and poured into the ear of night a flood of delicious melody. Hearing this, Babe seized Chichester's hat, and placed it on her head.

"There must be some omen in that," said Chichester.

"They say," said Babe, laughing merrily, "that ef a gal puts on a man's hat when she hears a mocker sing at night, she'll git married that year an' do well."

"Well, I'm sorry I haven't got a bonnet to put on," exclaimed Chichester.

"Oh, it don't work that away!" cried Babe.

The mocking-bird continued to sing, and finally brought its concert to a close by giving a most marvellous imitation of the liquid, silvery chimes of the wood-thrush.

There was a silence for one brief moment. Then there was a red flash under the apple-trees, followed by the sharp crack of a rifle. There was another brief moment of silence, and then the young girl sighed softly, leaned forward, and fell from her chair.

"What's this?" cried Abe, coming to the door.

"The Lord only knows!" exclaimed Chichester. "Look at your daughter!"

Abe stepped forward, and touched the girl on the shoulder. Then he shook her gently, as he had done a thousand times when rousing her from sleep.

"Babe! git up! Git up, honey, an' go in the house. You ought to 'a' been abed long ago. Git up, honey."

Chichester stood like one paralyzed. For the moment he was incapable of either speech or action.

"I know what she's atter," said Abe tenderly. "You wouldn't believe it skacely, but this yer great big chunk of a gal wants her ole pappy to pick her up an' tote her thes like he useter when she was er little bit of a scrap."

"I think she has been shot," said Chichester. To his own ears his voice seemed to be the voice of some other man.

"Shot!" exclaimed Abe. "Why, who's a-gwine to shoot Babe? Lord, Cap'n! you dunner nothin' 'tall 'bout Babe ef you talk that away. — Come on, honey." With that Abe lifted his child in his arms, and carried her into the house. Chichester followed. All his faculties were benumbed, and he seemed to be walking in a dream. It seemed that no such horrible confusion as that by which he was surrounded could have the remotest relation to reality.

Nevertheless, it did not add to his surprise and consternation to find, when Abe had placed the girl on her bed, that she was dead. A little red spot on her forehead, half-hidden by the glossy curling hair, showed that whoever held the rifle aimed it well.

"Why, honey," said Abe, wiping away the slight blood-stain that showed itself, "you struck your head ag'in' a nail. Git up! you oughtn't to be a-gwine on this away before comp'ny."

"I tell you she is dead!" cried Chichester. "She has been murdered!"

The girl's mother had already realized this fact, and her tearless grief was something pitiful to behold. The gray-haired grandfather had also realized it.

"I'd druther see her a-lyin' thar dead," he exclaimed, raising his weak and trembling hands heavenward, "than to see her Tuck Peevy's wife."

"Why, gentermen!" exclaimed Abe, "how *kin* she be dead? I oughter know my own gal, I reckon. Many's an' many's the time she's worried me, a-playin' 'possum, an' many's an' many's the time has I sot by her waitin' tell she let on to wake up. Don't you all pester wi' her. She'll wake up therreckly."

At this juncture Tuck Peevy walked into the room. There was a strange glitter in his eyes, a new energy in his movements. Chichester sprang at him, seized him by the throat, and dragged him to the bedside.

"You cowardly, skulking murderer!" he exclaimed, "see what you have done!"

Peevy's sallow face grew ashen. He seemed to shrink and collapse under Chichester's hand. His breath came thick and short. His long, bony fingers clutched nervously at his clothes.

"I aimed at the hat!" he exclaimed huskily.

He would have leaned over the girl, but Chichester flung him away from the bedside, and he sank down in a corner, moaning and shaking. Abe took no notice of Peevy's entrance, and paid no attention to the crouching figure mumbling in the corner, except, perhaps, so far as he seemed to recognize in Chichester's attack on Peevy a somewhat vigorous protest against his own theory; for, when there was comparative quiet in the room, Hightower raised himself, and exclaimed, in a tone that showed both impatience and excitement, —

"Why, great God A'mighty, gentermen, don't go on that away! They hain't no harm done. Thes let us alone. Me an' Babe's all right. She's bin a-playin' this away ev'ry sence she wuz a little bit of a gal. Don't less make her mad, gentermen, bekaze ef we do she'll take plum tell day atter to-morrer for to come 'roun' right."

Looking closely at Hightower, Chichester could see that his face was colorless. His eyes were sunken, but shone with a peculiar brilliancy, and great beads of perspiration stood on his forehead. His whole appearance was that of a man distraught. Here was another tragedy!

Seeking a momentary escape from the confusion and perplexity into which he had been plunged by the horrible events of the night, Chichester passed out into the yard, and stood bareheaded in the cool wind that was faintly stirring among the trees. The stars shone remote and tranquil, and the serenity of the mountain, the awful silence that seemed to be, not the absence of sound, but the presence of some spiritual entity, gave assurance of peace. Out there, in the cold air, or in the wide skies, or in the vast gulf of night, there was nothing to suggest either pity or compassion, — only the mysterious tranquillity of nature.

This was the end, so far as Chichester knew. He never entered the Hightower house again. Something prompted him to saddle his horse and ride down the mountain. The tragedy and its attendant troubles were never reported in the newspapers. The peace of the mountain remained undisturbed, its silence unbroken.

But should Chichester, who at last accounts was surveying a line of railway in Mexico, ever return to Lost Mountain, he would find Tuck Peevy a gaunt and shrunken creature, working on the Hightower farm, and managing such of its small affairs as call for management. Sometimes, when the day's work is over, and Peevy sits at the fireside saying nothing, Abe Hightower will raise a paralytic hand, and cry out as loud as he can that it's almost time for Babe to quit playing 'possum. At such times we may be sure that, so far as Peevy is concerned, there is still trouble on Lost Mountain.

AZALIA.

I.

MISS HELEN OSBORNE EUSTIS of Boston
was very much astonished one day in the early
fall of 1873 to receive a professional visit from Dr.
Ephraim Buxton, who for many years had been her
father's family physician. The astonishment was
mutual; for Dr. Buxton had expected to find Miss
Eustis in bed, or at least in the attitude of a patient,
whereas she was seated in an easy-chair, before a
glowing grate, — which the peculiarities of the Boston climate sometimes render necessary, even in the
early fall, — and appeared to be about as comfortable
as a human being could well be. Perhaps the appearance of comfort was heightened by the general
air of subdued luxury that pervaded the apartment
into which Dr. Buxton had been ushered. The
draperies, the arrangement of the little affairs that
answer to the name of bric-à-brac, the adjustment of
the furniture — every thing — conveyed the impression of peace and repose; and the chief element of
this perfect harmony was Miss Eustis herself, who
rose to greet the doctor as he entered. She re-

garded the physician with eyes that somehow seemed to be wise and kind, and with a smile that was at once sincere and humorous.

"Why, how is this, Helen?" Dr. Buxton exclaimed, taking off his spectacles, and staring at the young lady. "I fully expected to find you in bed. I hope you are not imprudent."

"Why should I be ill, Dr. Buxton? You know what Mr. Tom Appleton says: 'In Boston, those who are sick do injustice to the air they breathe and to their cooks.' I think that is a patriotic sentiment, and I try to live up to it. My health is no worse than usual, and usually it is very good," said Miss Eustis.

"You certainly seem to be well," said Dr. Buxton, regarding the young lady with a professional frown; "but appearances are sometimes deceitful. I met Harriet yesterday" —

"Ah, my aunt!" exclaimed Helen, in a tone calculated to imply that this explained every thing.

"I met Harriet yesterday, and she insisted on my coming to see you at once, certainly not later than to-day."

Miss Eustis shrugged her shoulders, and laughed, but her face showed that she appreciated this manifestation of solicitude.

"Let me see," she said reflectively; "what was my complaint yesterday? We must do justice to Aunt Harriet's discrimination. She would never forgive you if you went away without leaving a prescription. My health is so good that I think you may leave me a mild one."

Unconsciously the young lady made a charming picture as she sat with·her head drooping a little to one side in a half-serious, half-smiling effort to recall to mind some of the symptoms that had excited her aunt's alarm. Dr. Buxton, prescription-book in hand, gazed at her quizzically over his old-fashioned spectacles; seeing which, Helen laughed heartily. At that moment her aunt entered the room, — a pleasant-faced but rather prim old lady, of whom it had been said by some one competent to judge, that her inquisitiveness was so overwhelming and so important that it took the shape of pity in one direction, patriotism in another, and benevolence in another, giving to her life not the mere semblance but the very essence of usefulness and activity.

"Do you hear that, Dr. Buxton?" cried the pleasant-faced old lady somewhat sharply. "Do you hear her wheeze when she laughs? Do you remember that she was threatened with pneumonia last winter? and now she is wheezing before the winter begins!"

"This is the trouble I was trying to think of," exclaimed Helen, sinking back in her chair with a gesture of mock despair.

"Don't make yourself ridiculous, dear," said the aunt, giving the little clusters of gray curls that

hung about her ears an emphatic shake. " Serious
matters should be taken seriously." Whereat Helen
pressed her cheek gently against the thin white hand
that had been laid caressingly on her shoulder.

" Aunt Harriet has probably heard me say that there
is still some hope for the country, even though it is
governed entirely by men," said Helen, with an air of
apology. " The men cannot deprive us of the winter
climate of Boston, and I enjoy that above all things."

Aunt Harriet smiled reproachfully at her niece,
and pulled her ear gently.

"But indeed, Dr. Buxton," Helen went on more
seriously, "the winter climate of Boston, fine as it is,
is beginning to pinch us harder than it used to do.
The air is thinner, and the cold is keener. When I
was younger — very much younger — than I am now,
I remember that I used to run in and out, and fall
and roll in the snow with perfect impunity. But now
I try to profit by Aunt Harriet's example. When I
go out, I go bundled up to the point of suffocation ;
and if the wind is from the east, as it usually is, I
wear wraps and shawls indoors."

Helen smiled brightly at her aunt and at Dr.
Buxton ; but her aunt seemed to be distressed, and
the physician shook his head dubiously.

"You will have to take great care of yourself,"
said Dr. Buxton. "You must be prudent. The
slightest change in the temperature may send you
to bed for the rest of the winter."

"Dr. Buxton is complimenting you, Aunt Harriet," said Helen. "You should drop him a courtesy."

Whereupon the amiable physician, seeing that there was no remedy for the humorous view which Miss Eustis took of her condition, went further, and informed her that there was every reason why she should be serious. He told her, with some degree of bluntness, that her symptoms, while not alarming, were not at all re-assuring.

"It is always the way, Dr. Buxton," said Helen, smiling tenderly at her aunt; "I believe you would confess to serious symptoms yourself if Aunt Harriet insisted on it. What an extraordinary politician she would make! My sympathy with the woman-suffrage movement is in the nature of an investment. When we women succeed to the control of affairs, I count on achieving distinction as Aunt Harriet's niece."

Laughing, she seized her aunt's hand. Dr. Buxton, watching her, laughed too, and then proceeded to write out a prescription. He seemed to hesitate a little over this; seeing which, Helen remonstrated, —

"Pray Dr. Buxton, don't humor Aunt Harriet too much in this. Save your physic for those who are strong in body and mind. A dozen of your pellets ought to be a year's supply." The physician wrote out his prescription, and took his leave, laughing heartily at the amiable confusion in which Helen's drollery had left her aunt.

It is not to be supposed, however, that Miss Eustis was simply droll. She was unconventional at all times, and sometimes wilful, — inheriting that native strength of mind and mother-wit which are generally admitted to be a part of the equipment of the typical American woman. If she was not the ideal young woman, at least she possessed some of the attractive qualities that one tries — sometimes unsuccessfully — to discover in one's dearest friends. From her infancy, until near the close of the war, she had had the advantage of her father's companionship, so that her ideas were womanly rather than merely feminine. She had never been permitted to regard the world from the dormer-windows of a young ladies' seminary, in consequence of which her views of life in general, and of mankind in particular, were orderly and rational. Such indulgence as her father had given her had served to strengthen her individuality rather than to confirm her temper; and, though she had a strong and stubborn will of her own, her tact was such that her wilfulness appeared to be the most natural as well as the most charming thing in the world. Moreover, she possessed in a remarkable degree that buoyancy of mind that is more engaging than mere geniality.

Her father was no less a person than Charles Osborne Eustis, the noted philanthropist and abolitionist, whose death in 1867 was the occasion of quite a controversy in New England, — a contro-

versy based on the fact that he had opposed some
of the most virulent schemes of his co-workers at a
time when abolitionism had not yet gathered its full
strength. Mr. Eustis, in his day, was in the habit
of boasting that his daughter had a great deal of
genuine American spirit, — the spirit that one set
of circumstances drives to provinciality, another to
patriotism, and another to originality.

Helen had spent two long winters in Europe
without parting with the fine flavor of her originality. She was exceedingly modest in her designs,
too, for she went neither as a missionary nor as a
repentant. She found no foreign social shrines that
she thought worthy of worshipping at. She admired
what was genuine, and tolerated such shams as ob-
truded themselves on her attention. Her father's
connections had enabled her to see something of the
real home-life of England; and she was delighted,
but not greatly surprised, to find that at its best it
was not greatly different from the home-life to which
she had been accustomed.

The discovery delighted her because it confirmed
her own broad views; but she no more thought it
necessary to set about aping the social peculiarities
to be found in London drawing-rooms than she
thought of denying her name or her nativity. She
made many interesting studies and comparisons, but
she was not disposed to be critical. She admired
many things in Europe which she would not have

considered admirable in America, and whatever she
found displeasing she tolerated as the natural outcome of social or climatic conditions. Certainly the
idea never occurred to her that her own country was
a barren waste because time had not set the seal of
antiquity on its institutions. On the other hand,
this admirable young woman was quick to perceive
that much information as well as satisfaction was to
be obtained by regarding various European peculiarities from a strictly European point of view.

But Miss Eustis's reminiscences of the Old World
were sad as well as pleasant. Her journey thither
had been undertaken in the hope of restoring her
father's failing health, and her stay there had been
prolonged for the same purpose. For a time he
grew stronger and better, but the improvement was
only temporary. He came home to die, and to
Helen this result seemed to be the end of all things.
She had devoted herself to looking after his comfort with a zeal and an intelligence that left nothing
undone. This had been her mission in life. Her
mother had died when Helen was a little child,
leaving herself and her brother, who was some years
older, to the care of the father. Helen remembered
her mother only as a pale, beautiful lady in a trailing
robe, who fell asleep one day, and was mysteriously
carried away, — the lady of a dream.

The boy — the brother — rode forth to the war in
1862, and never rode back any more. To the father

and sister waiting at home, it seemed as if he had been seized and swept from the earth on the bosom of the storm that broke over the country in that period of dire confusion. Even Rumor, with her thousand tongues, had little to say of the fate of this poor youth. It was known that he led a squad of troopers detailed for special service, and that his command, with small knowledge of the country, fell into an ambush from which not more than two or three extricated themselves. Beyond this all was mystery, for those who survived that desperate skirmish could say nothing of the fate of their companions. The loss of his son gave Mr. Eustis additional interest in his daughter, if that were possible; and the common sorrow of the two so strengthened and sweetened their lives, that their affection for each other was in the nature of a perpetual memorial of the pale lady who had passed away, and of the boy who had perished in Virginia.

When Helen's father died, in 1867, her mother's sister, Miss Harriet Tewksbury, a spinster of fifty or thereabouts, who, for the lack of something substantial to interest her, had been halting between woman's rights and Spiritualism, suddenly discovered that Helen's cause was the real woman's cause; whereupon she went to the lonely and grief-stricken girl, and with that fine efficiency which the New-England woman acquires from the air, and inherits from history, proceeded to minister to her comfort.

Miss Tewksbury was not at all vexed to find her niece capable of taking care of herself. She did not allow that fact to prevent her from assuming a motherly control that was most gracious in its manifestations, and peculiarly gratifying to Helen, who found great consolation in the all-but masculine energy of her aunt.

A day or two after Dr. Buxton's visit, the result of which has already been chronicled, Miss Tewksbury's keen eye detected an increase of the symptoms that had given her anxiety, and their development was of such a character that Helen made no objection when her aunt proposed to call in the physician again. Dr. Buxton came, and agreed with Miss Tewksbury as to the gravity of the symptoms; but his prescription was oral.

"You must keep Helen indoors until she is a little stronger," he said to Miss Tewksbury, "and then take her to a milder climate."

"Oh, not to Florida!" exclaimed Helen promptly.

"Not necessarily," said the doctor.

"Please don't twist your language, Dr. Buxton. You should say necessarily not."

"And why not to Florida, young lady?" the doctor inquired.

"Ah, I have seen people that came from there," said Helen : "they were too tired to talk much about the country, but something in their attitude and appearance seemed to suggest that they had seen the

sea-serpent. Dear doctor, I have no desire to see
the sea-serpent."

"Well, then, my dear child," said Dr. Buxton
soothingly, "not to Florida, but to nature's own
sanitarium, the pine woods of Georgia. Yes," the
doctor went on, smiling as he rubbed the glasses of
his spectacles with his silk handkerchief, "nature's
own sanitarium. I tested the piney woods of Georgia
thoroughly years ago. I drifted there in my young
days. I lived there, and taught school there. I grew
strong there, and I have always wanted to go back
there."

"And now," said Helen, with a charmingly demure
glance at the enthusiastic physician, "you want to
send Aunt Harriet and poor Me forward as a skir-
mish-line. There is no antidote in your books for
the Ku Klux."

"You will see new scenes and new people," said
Dr. Buxton, laughing. "You will get new ideas;
above all, you will breathe the fresh air of heaven
spiced with the odor of pines. It will be the making
of you, my dear child."

Helen made various protests, some of them serious
and some droll, but the matter was practically settled when it became evident that Dr. Buxton was
not only earnestly but enthusiastically in favor of
the journey; and Helen's aunt at once began to
make preparations. To some of their friends it
seemed a serious undertaking indeed. The news-

papers of that day were full of accounts of Ku-Klux
outrages, and of equally terrible reports of the social
disorganization of the South. It seemed at that time
as though the politicians and the editors, both great
and small, and of every shade of belief, had determined to fight the war over again, — instituting a
conflict which, though bloodless enough so far as
the disputants were concerned, was not without its
unhappy results.

Moreover, Helen's father had been noted among
those who had early engaged in the crusade against
slavery; and it was freely predicted by her friends
that the lawlessness which was supposed to exist
in every part of the collapsed Confederacy would
be prompt to select the representatives of Charles
Osborne Eustis as its victims. Miss Tewksbury
affected to smile at the apprehensions of her friends,
but her preparations were not undertaken without a
secret dread of the responsibilities she was assuming.
Helen, however, was disposed to treat the matter
humorously.

"Dr. Buxton is a lifelong Democrat," she said;
"consequently he must know all about it. Father
used to tell him he liked his medicine better than
his politics, bitter as some of it was; but in a case
of this kind, Dr. Buxton's politics have a distinct
value. He will give us the grips, the signs, and the
pass-words, dear aunt, and I dare say we shall get
along comfortably."

II.

THEY did get along comfortably. Peace seemed
to spread her meshes before them. They journeyed
by easy stages, stopping a while in Philadephia, in
Baltimore, and in Washington. They staid a week
in Richmond. From Richmond they were to go to
Atlanta, and from Atlanta to Azalia, the little piney-
woods village which Dr. Buxton had recommended
as a sanitarium. At a point south of Richmond,
where they stopped for breakfast, Miss Eustis and
her aunt witnessed a little scene that seemed to
them to be very interesting. A gentleman wrapped
in a long linen travelling-coat was pacing restlessly
up and down the platform of the little station. He
was tall, and his bearing was distinctly military.
The neighborhood people who were lounging around
the station watched him with interest. After a
while a negro boy came running up with a valise
which he had evidently brought some distance. He
placed it in front of the tall gentleman, crying out
in a loud voice, "Here she is, Marse Peyton," then
stepped to one side, and began to fan himself vigorously with the fragment of a wool hat. He grinned
broadly in response to something the tall gentleman
said; but, before he could make a suitable reply, a
negro woman, fat and motherly-looking, made her
appearance, puffing and blowing and talking.

"I declar' ter gracious, Marse Peyton! seem like
I wa'n't never gwine ter git yer. I helt up my
head, I did, fer ter keep my eye on de kyars, en it
look like I run inter all de gullies en on top er all
de stumps 'twix' dis en Marse Tip's. I des tuk'n
drapt eve'y thing, I did, en tole um dey'd hatter
keep one eye on de dinner-pot, kase I 'blige ter run
en see Marse Peyton off."

The gentleman laughed as the motherly-looking
old negro wiped her face with her apron. Her sleeves
were rolled up, and her fat arms glistened in the sun.

"I boun' you some er deze yer folks 'll go off en
say I'm 'stracted," she cried, "but I can't he'p dat;
I bleeze ter run down yer ter tell Marse Peyton good-
by. Tell um all howdy fer me, Marse Peyton," she
cried, "all un um. No diffunce ef I ain't know um
all — 'tain't gwine ter do no harm fer ter tell um dat
ole Jincy say howdy. Hit make me feel right foolish
in de head w'en it come 'cross me dat I use ter tote
Miss Hallie 'roun' w'en she wuz a little bit er baby,
en now she way down dar out'n de worl' mos'. I
wish ter de Lord I uz gwine 'long wid you, Marse
Peyton! Yit I speck, time I got dar, I'd whirl in en
wish myse'f back home."

The negro boy carried the gentleman's valise into
the sleeping-coach, and placed it opposite the seats
occupied by Helen and her aunt. Across the end
was stencilled in white the name " Peyton Garwood."
When the train was ready to start, the gentleman

shook hands with the negro woman and with the boy. The woman seemed to be very much affected.

"God A'mighty bless you, Marse Peyton, honey!" she exclaimed as the train moved off; and as long as Helen could see her, she was waving her hands in farewell. Both Helen and her aunt had watched this scene with considerable interest, and now, when the gentleman had been escorted to his seat by the obsequious porter, they regarded him with some curiosity. He appeared to be about thirty-five years old. His face would have been called exceedingly handsome, but for a scar on his right cheek; and yet, on closer inspection, the scar seemed somehow to fit the firm outlines of his features. His brown beard emphasized the strength of his chin. His nose was slightly aquiline, his eyebrows were a trifle rugged, and his hair was brushed straight back from a high forehead. His face was that of a man who had seen rough service and had enjoyed it keenly, — a face full of fire and resolution, with some subtle suggestion of tenderness.

"She called him 'Master,' Helen," said Miss Tewksbury after a while, referring to the scene at the station; "did you hear her?" Miss Tewksbury's tone implied wrathfulness that was too sure of its own justification to assert itself noisily.

"I heard her," Helen replied. "She called him Master, and he called her Mammy. It was a very pleasing exchange of compliments."

Such further comment as the ladies may have felt called on to make — for it was a matter in which both were very much interested — was postponed for the time being. A passenger occupying a seat in the farther end of the coach had recognized the gentleman whose valise was labelled "Peyton Garwood," and now pressed forward to greet him. This passenger was a very aggressive-looking person. He was short and stout, but there was no suggestion of jollity or even of good humor in his rotundity. No one would have made the mistake of alluding to him as a fat man. He would have been characterized as the pudgy man ; and even his pudginess was aggressive. He had evidently determined to be dignified at any cost, but his seriousness seemed to be perfectly gratuitous.

"Gener'l Garwood?" he said in an impressive tone, as he leaned over the tall gentleman's seat.

"Ah! Goolsby!" exclaimed the other, extending his hand. "Why, how do you do? Sit down."

Goolsby's pudginess became more apparent and apparently more aggressive than ever when he seated himself near Gen. Garwood.

"Well, sir, I can't say my health's any too good. You look mighty well yourse'f, gener'l. How are things?" said Goolsby, pushing his travelling-cap over his eyes, and frowning as if in pain.

"Oh, affairs seem to be improving," Gen. Garwood replied.

"Well, now, I ain't so up and down certain about that, gener'l," said Goolsby, settling himself back, and frowning until his little eyes disappeared. "Looks like to me that things git wuss and wuss. I ain't no big man, and I'm ruther disj'inted when it comes right down to politics ; but blame me if it don't look to me mighty like the whole of creation is driftin' 'round loose."

"Ah, well," said the general soothingly, "a great many things are uncomfortable ; there is a good deal of unnecessary irritation growing out of new and unexpected conditions. But we are getting along better than we are willing to admit. We are all fond of grumbling."

"That's so," said Goolsby, with the air of a man who is willing to make any sacrifice for the sake of a discussion ; "that's so. But I tell you we're havin' mighty tough times, gener'l, — mighty tough times. Yonder's the Yankees on one side, and here's the blamed niggers on t'other, and betwixt and betweenst 'em a white man's got mighty little chance. And then, right on top of the whole caboodle, here comes the panic in the banks, and the epizooty 'mongst the cattle. I tell you, gener'l, it's tough times, and it's in-about as much as an honest man can do to pay hotel bills and have a ticket ready to show up when the conductor comes along."

Gen. Garwood smiled sympathetically, and Goolsby went on : —

"Here I've been runnin' up and down the country tryin' to sell a book, and I ain't sold a hunderd copies sence I started,— no, sir, not a hunderd copies. Maybe you'd like to look at it, gener'l," continued Goolsby, stiffening up a little. "If I do say it my-self, it's in-about the best book that a man'll git a chance to thumb in many a long day."

"What book is it, Goolsby?" the general inquired.

Goolsby sprang up, waddled rapidly to where he had left his satchel, and returned, bringing a large and substantial-looking volume.

"It's a book that speaks for itself any day in the week," he said, running the pages rapidly between his fingers; "it's a history of our own great conflict, — 'The Rise and Fall of the Rebellion,' by Schuyler Paddleford. I don't know what the blamed publish-ers wanted to put it 'Rebellion' for. I told 'em, says I, 'Gentlemen, it'll be up-hill work with this in the Sunny South. Call it "The Conflict,"' says I. But they wouldn't listen, and now I have to work like a blind nigger splittin' rails. But she's a daisy, gener'l, as shore as you're born. She jess reads right straight along from cover to cover without a bobble. Why, sir, I never know'd what war was till I mean-dered through the sample pages of this book. And they've got your picture in here, gener'l, jest as natural as life, — all for five dollars in cloth, eight in liberry style, and ten in morocker."

Gen. Garwood glanced over the specimen pages

with some degree of interest, while Goolsby continued to talk.

"Now, betwixt you and me, gener'l," he went on confidentially, "I don't nigh like the style of that book, particular where it rattles up our side. I wa'n't in the war myself, but blame me if it don't rile me when I hear outsiders a-cussin' them that was. I come mighty nigh not takin' holt of it on that account; but 'twouldn't have done no good, not a bit. If sech a book is got to be circulated around here, it better be circulated by some good Southron, — a man that's a kind of antidote to the pizen, as it were. If I don't sell it, some blamed Yankee'll jump in and gallop around with it. And I tell you what, gener'l, betwixt you and me and the gate-post, it's done come to that pass where a man can't afford to be too plegged particular; if he stops for to scratch his head and consider whether he's a gentleman, some other feller'll jump in and snatch the rations right out of his mouth. That's why I'm a-paradin' around tryin' to sell this book."

"Well," said Gen. Garwood in an encouraging tone, "I have no doubt it is a very interesting book. I have heard of it before. Fetch me a copy when you come to Azalia again."

Goolsby smiled an unctuous and knowing smile.

"Maybe you think I ain't a-comin'," he exclaimed, with the air of a man who has invented a joke that he relishes. "Well, sir, you're getting the wrong measure. I was down in 'Zalia Monday was a week, and I'm a-goin' down week after next. Fact is," continued Goolsby, rather sheepishly, "'Zalia is a mighty nice place. Gener'l, do you happen to know Miss Louisa Hornsby? Of course you do! Well, sir, you might go a week's journey in the wildwood, as the poet says, and not find a handsomer gal then that. She's got style from away back."

"Why, yes!" exclaimed the general in a tone of hearty congratulation, "of course I know Miss Lou. She is a most excellent young lady. And so the wind sits in that quarter? Your blushes, Goolsby, are a happy confirmation of many sweet and piquant rumors."

Goolsby appeared to be very much embarrassed. He moved about uneasily in his seat, searched in all his pockets for something or other that wasn't there, and made a vain effort to protest. He grew violently red in the face, and the vivid color gleamed through his closely cropped hair.

"Oh, come now, gener'l!" he exclaimed. "Oh, pshaw! Why — oh, go 'way!"

His embarrassment was so great, and seemed to border so closely on epilepsy, that the general was induced to offer him a cigar and invite him into the smoking-apartment. As Gėn. Garwood and Goolsby passed out, Helen Eustis drew a long breath.

"It is worth the trouble of a long journey to behold such a spectacle," she declared. Her aunt regarded her curiously. "Who would have thought it?" she went on, — "a Southern secessionist charged with affability, and a book-agent radiant with embarrassment!"

"He is a coarse, ridiculous creature," said Miss Tewksbury sharply.

"The affable general, Aunt Harriet?"

"No, child; the other."

"Dear aunt, we are in the enemy's country, and we must ground our prejudices. The book-agent is pert and crude, but he is not coarse. A coarse man may be in love, but he would never blush over it. And as for the affable general — you saw the negro woman cry over him."

"Poor thing!" said Miss Tewksbury, with a sigh. "She sadly needs Instruction."

"Ah, yes! that is a theory we should stand to, but how shall we instruct her to run and cry after us?"

"My dear child, we want no such disgusting exhibitions. It is enough if we do our duty by these unfortunates."

"But I do want just such an exhibition, Aunt Harriet," said Helen seriously. "I should be glad to have some fortunate or unfortunate creature run and cry after me."

"Well," said Miss Tewksbury placidly, "we are about to ignore the most impressive fact, after all."

"What is that, Aunt Harriet?"

"Why, child, these people are from Azalia, and for us Azalia is the centre of the universe."

"Ah, don't pretend that you are not charmed, dear aunt. We shall have the pleasure of meeting the handsome Miss Hornsby, and probably Mr. Goolsby himself — and certainly the distinguished general."

"I only hope Ephraim Buxton has a clear conscience to-day," remarked Miss Tewksbury with unction.

"Did you observe the attitude of the general towards Mr. Goolsby, and that of Mr. Goolsby towards the general?" asked Helen, ignoring the allusion to Dr. Buxton. "The line that the general drew was visible to the naked eye. But Mr. Goolsby drew no line. He is friendly and familiar on principle. I was reminded of the 'Brookline Reporter,' which alluded the other day to the London 'Times' as its esteemed contemporary. The affable general is Mr. Goolsby's esteemed contemporary."

"My dear child," said Miss Tewksbury, somewhat anxiously, "I hope your queer conceits are not the result of your illness."

"No, they are the result of my surroundings. I have been trying to pretend to myself, ever since we left Washington, that we are travelling through a strange country; but it is a mere pretence. I have been trying to verify some previous impressions of barbarism and shiftlessness."

"Well, upon my word, my dear," exclaimed Miss Tewksbury, "I should think you had had ample opportunity."

"I have been trying to take the newspaper view," Helen went on with some degree of earnestness, "but it is impossible. We must correct the newspapers, Aunt Harriet, and make ourselves famous. Every thing I have seen that is not to be traced to the result of the war belongs to a state of arrested development."

Miss Tewksbury was uncertain whether her niece was giving a new turn to her drollery, so she merely stared at her; but the young lady seemed to be serious enough.

"Don't interrupt me, Aunt Harriet. Give me the opportunity you would give to Dr. Barlow Blade, the trance medium. Every thing I see in this country belongs to a state of arrested development, and it has been arrested at a most interesting point. It is picturesque. It is colonial. I am amazed that this fact has not been dwelt on by people who write about the South."

"The conservatism that prevents progress, or stands in the way of it, is a crime," said Miss Tewksbury, pressing her thin lips together firmly. She had once been on the platform in some of the little country towns of New England, and had made quite a reputation for pith and fluency.

"Ah, dear aunt, that sounds like an extract from a

lecture. We can have progress in some things, but not in others. We have progressed in the matter of conveniences, comforts, and luxuries, but in what other directions? Are we any better than the people who lived in the days of Washington, Jefferson, and Madison? Is the standard of morality any higher now than it was in the days of the apostles?"

"Don't talk nonsense, Helen," said Miss Tewksbury. "We have a higher civilization than the apostles witnessed. Morality is progressive."

"Well," said Helen, with a sigh, "it is a pity these people have discarded shoe-buckles and knee-breeches."

"Your queer notions make me thirsty, child," said Miss Tewksbury, producing a silver cup from her satchel. "I must get a drink of water."

"Permit me, madam," said a sonorous voice behind them ; and a tall gentleman seized the cup, and bore it away.

"It is the distinguished general!" exclaimed Helen in a tragic whisper, "and he must have heard our speeches."

"I hope he took them down," said Miss Tewksbury snappishly. "He will esteem you as a sympathizer."

"Did I say any thing ridiculous, aunt Harriet?"

"Dear me! you must ask your distinguished general," replied Miss Tewksbury triumphantly.

Gen. Garwood returned with the water, and in-

sisted on fetching more.   Helen observed that he
held his hat in his hand, and that his attitude was
one of unstudied deference.

"The conductor tells me, madam," he said, addressing himself to Miss Tewksbury, "that you
have tickets for Azalia.   I am going in that direction myself, and I should be glad to be of any
service to you.   Azalia is a poor little place, but I
like it well enough to live there.   I suppose that is
the reason the conductor told me of your tickets.
He knew the information would be interesting."

"Thank you," said Miss Tewksbury with dignity.

"You are very kind," said Miss Eustis with a
smile.

Gen. Garwood made himself exceedingly agreeable.   He pointed out the interesting places along
the road, gave the ladies little bits of local history
that were at least entertaining.   In Atlanta, where
there was a delay of a few hours, he drove them
over the battle-fields, and by his graphic descrip-
tions gave them a new idea of the heat and fury of
war.   In short, he made himself so agreeable in
every way that Miss Tewksbury felt at liberty to
challenge his opinions on various subjects.   They
had numberless little controversies about the rights
and wrongs of the war, and the perplexing problems that grew out of its results.   So far as Miss
Tewksbury was concerned, she found Gen. Garwood's
large tolerance somewhat irritating, for it left her

no excuse for the employment of her most effective arguments.

"Did you surrender your prejudices at Appomattox?" Miss Tewksbury asked him on one occasion.

"Oh, by no means; you remember we were allowed to retain our side-arms and our saddle-horses," he replied, laughing. "I still have my prejudices, but I trust they are more important than those I entertained in my youth. Certainly they are less uncomfortable."

"Well," said Miss Tewksbury, "you are still unrepentant, and that is more serious than any number of prejudices."

"There is nothing to repent of," said the general, smiling, a little sadly as Helen thought. "It has all passed away utterly. The best we can do is that which seems right and just and necessary. My duty was as plain to me in 1861, when I was a boy of twenty, as it is to-day. It seemed to be my duty then to serve my State and section; my duty now seems to be to help good people everywhere to restore the Union, and to heal the wounds of the war."

"I'm *very* glad to hear you say so," exclaimed Miss Tewksbury in a tone that made Helen shiver. "I was afraid it was quite otherwise. It seems to me, that, if I lived here, I should either hate the people who conquered me, or else the sin of slavery would weigh heavily on my conscience."

"I can appreciate that feeling, I think," said Gen. Garwood, "but the American conscience is a very healthy one, — not likely to succumb to influences that are mainly malarial in their nature ; and even from your point of view some good can be found in American slavery."

"I have never found it," said Miss Tewksbury.

"You must admit that but for slavery the negroes who are here would be savages in Africa. As it is, they have had the benefit of more than two hundred years' contact with the white race. If they are at all fitted for citizenship, the result is due to the civilizing influence of slavery. It seems to me that they are vastly better off as American citizens, even though they have endured the discipline of slavery, than they would be as savages in Africa."

Miss Tewksbury's eyes snapped. "Did this make slavery right?" she asked.

"Not at all," said the general, smiling at the lady's earnestness. "But, at least, it is something of an excuse for American slavery. It seems to be an evidence that Providence had a hand in the whole unfortunate business."

But in spite of these discussions and controversies, the general made himself so thoroughly agreeable in every way, and was so thoughtful in his attentions, that by the time Helen and her aunt arrived at Azalia they were disposed to believe that he had placed them under many obligations, and

they said so; but the general insisted that it was
he who had been placed under obligations, and he
declared it to be his intention to discharge a few
of them as soon as the ladies found themselves
comfortably settled in the little town to which Dr.
Buxton had banished them.

III.

AZALIA was a small town, but it was a comparatively comfortable one. For years and years before
the war it had been noted as the meeting-place of the
wagon-trains by means of which the planters trans-
ported their produce to market. It was on the highway that led from the cotton-plantations of Middle
Georgia to the city of Augusta. It was also a stop-
ping-place for the stage-coaches that carried the
mails. Azalia was not a large town, even before the
war, when, according to the testimony of the entire
community, it was at its best; and it certainly had
not improved any since the war. There was room
for improvement, but no room for progress, because
there was no necessity for progress. The people
were contented. They were satisfied with things as
they existed, though they had an honest, provincial
faith in the good old times that were gone. They
had but one regret, — that the railroad-station, four
miles away, had been named Azalia. It is true, the
station consisted of a water-tank and a little pigeon-

house where tickets were sold; but the people of
Azalia proper felt that it was in the nature of an out-
rage to give so fine a name to so poor a place. They
derived some satisfaction, however, from the fact
that the world at large found it necessary to make
a distinction between the two places. Azalia was
called " Big Azalia," and the railroad-station was
known as " Little Azalia."

Away back in the forties, or perhaps even earlier,
when there was some excitement in all parts of the
country in regard to railroad-building, one of Georgia's most famous orators had alluded in the legisla-
ture to Azalia as " the natural gateway of the com-
merce of the Empire State of the South." This fine
phrase stuck in the memories of the people of Azalia
and their posterity; and the passing traveller, since
that day and time, has heard a good deal of it. There
is no doubt that the figure was fairly applicable
before the railways were built ; for, as has been explained, Azalia was the meeting-place of the wagon-
trains from all parts of the State in going to market.
When the cotton-laden wagons met at Azalia, they
parted company no more until they had reached
Augusta. The natural result of this was that Azalia,
in one way and another, saw a good deal of life, —
much that was entertaining, and a good deal that
was exciting. Another result was that the people
had considerable practice in the art of hospitality ;
for it frequently happened that the comfortable tav-

ern, which Azalia's commercial importance had made
necessary at a very early period of the town's history,
was full to overflowing with planters accompanying
their wagons, and lawyers travelling from court to
court.   At such times the worthy townspeople would
come to the rescue, and offer the shelter of their
homes to the belated wayfarer.

There was another feature of Azalia worthy of
attention.   It was in a measure the site and centre
of a mission, — the headquarters, so to speak, of a
very earnest and patient effort to infuse energy and
ambition into that indescribable class of people
known in that region as the piney-woods "Tackies."
Within a stone's-throw of Azalia there was a scat-
tering settlement of these Tackies.   They had settled there before the Revolution, and had remained
there ever since, unchanged and unchangeable,
steeped in poverty of the most desolate description,
and living the narrowest lives possible in this great
Republic.   They had attracted the attention of the
Rev. Arthur Hill, an Episcopalian minister, who
conceived an idea that the squalid settlement near
Azalia afforded a fine field for missionary labor.   Mr.
Hill established himself in Azalia, built and furnished
a little church in the settlement, and entered on a
career of the most earnest and persevering charity.
To all appearances his labor was thrown away ; but
he was possessed by both faith and hope, and never
allowed himself to be disheartened.   All his time, as

well as the modest fortune left him by his wife who was dead, was devoted to the work of improving and elevating the Tackies ; and he never permitted himself to doubt for an instant that reasonable success was crowning his efforts. He was gentle, patient, and somewhat finical.

This was the neighborhood towards which Miss Eustis and her aunt had journeyed. Fortunately for these ladies, Major Haley, the genial tavern-keeper, had a habit of sending a hack to meet every train that stopped at Little Azalia. It was not a profitable habit in the long-run ; but Major Haley thought little of the profits, so long as he was conscious that the casual traveller had abundant reason to be grateful to him. Major Haley himself was a native of Kentucky ; but his wife was a Georgian, inheriting her thrift and her economy from a generation that knew more about the hand-loom, the spinning-wheel, and the cotton-cards, than it did about the piano. She admired her husband, who was a large, fine-looking man, with jocular tendencies ; but she disposed of his opinions without ceremony when they came in conflict with her own. Under these circumstances it was natural that she should have charge of the tavern and all that appertained thereto.

Gen. Garwood, riding by from Little Azalia, whither his saddle-horse had been sent to meet him, had informed the major that two ladies from the North were coming in the hack, and begged him to make

them as comfortable as possible. This information
Major Haley dutifully carried to his wife.

"Good Lord!" exclaimed Mrs. Haley, "what do
you reckon they want here?"

" I've been a-studyin'," said her husband thought-
fully. "The gener'l says they're comin' fer their
health."

"Well, it's a mighty fur cry for health," said Mrs.
Haley emphatically. "I've seen some monst'ous
sick people around here; and if anybody'll look at
them Tackies out on the Ridge yonder, and then
tell me there's any health in this neighborhood,
then I'll give up. I don't know how in the wide
world we'll fix up for 'em. That everlastin' nigger
went and made too much fire in the stove, and tee-
totally ruint my light-bread; I could 'a' cried, I was
so mad; and then on top er that the whole dinin'-
room is tore up from top to bottom."

"Well," said the major, "we'll try and make
'em comfortable, and if they ain't comfortable it
won't be our fault. Jest you whirl in, and put on
some of your Greene County style, Maria. That'll
fetch 'em."

"It may fetch 'em, but it won't feed 'em," said
the practical Maria.

The result was, that when Helen Eustis and her
aunt became the guests of this poor little country
tavern, they were not only agreeably disappointed
as to their surroundings, but they were better

pleased than they would have been at one of the most pretentious caravansaries. Hotel luxury is comfortable enough to those who make it a point to appreciate what they pay for ; but the appointments of luxury can neither impart, nor compensate for the lack of, the atmosphere that mysteriously conveys some impression or reminiscence of home. In the case of Helen and her aunt, this impression was conveyed and confirmed by a quilt of curious pattern on one of the beds in their rooms.

" My dear," said Miss Tewksbury, after making a critical examination, "your grandmother had just such a quilt as this. Yes, she had two. I remember the first one was quite a bone of contention between your mother and me, and so your grandmother made two. I declare," Miss Tewksbury continued, with a sigh, "it quite carries me back to old times."

" It is well made," said Helen, giving the stitches a critical examination, " and the colors are perfectly matched. Really, this is something to think about, for it fits none of our theories. Perhaps, Aunt Harriet, we have accidentally discovered some of our long-lost relatives. It would be nice and original to substitute a beautiful quilt for the ordinary strawberry-mark."

" Well, the sight of it is comforting, anyhow," said Miss Tewksbury, responding to the half-serious humor of her niece by pressing her thin lips together, and tossing her gray ringlets.

As she spoke, a negro boy, apparently about ten years old, stalked unceremoniously into the room, balancing a large stone pitcher on his head. His hands were tucked beneath his white apron, and the pitcher seemed to be in imminent danger of falling; but he smiled and showed his white teeth.

"I come fer ter fetch dish yer pitcher er water, ma'm. Miss 'Ria say she speck you lak fer have 'im right fresh from de well."

"Aren't you afraid you'll drop it?" said Miss Eustis.

"Lor', no'm!" exclaimed the boy, emphasizing his words by increasing his grin. "I been ca'um dis away sence I ain't no bigger dan my li'l' buddy. Miss 'Ria, she say dat w'at make I so bow-legged."

"What is your name?" inquired Miss Tewksbury, with some degree of solemnity, as the boy deposited the pitcher on the wash-stand.

"Mammy she say I un name Willum, but Mars Maje en de turrer folks dey des calls me Bill. I run'd off en sot in de school-'ouse all day one day, but dat mus' 'a' been a mighty bad day, kaze I ain't never year um say wherrer I wuz name Willum, er wherrer I wuz des name Bill. Miss 'Ria, she say dat 'tain't make no diffunce w'at folks' name is, long ez dey come w'en dey year turrer folks holl'in' at um."

"Don't you go to school, child?" Miss Tewks-bury inquired, with dignified sympathy.

"I start in once," said William, laughing, "but mos' time I git dar de nigger man w'at do de teachin' tuck'n snatch de book out'n my han' en say I got 'im upper-side down. I tole 'im dat de onliest way w'at I kin git my lesson, en den dat nigger man tuck'n lam me side de head. Den atter school bin turn out, I is hide myse'f side de road, en w'en dat nigger man come 'long, I up wid a rock en I fetched 'im a clip dat mighty nigh double 'im up. You ain't never is year no nigger man holler lak dat nigger man. He run'd en tole Mars Peyt dat de Kukluckers wuz atter 'im. Mars Peyt he try ter quile 'im, but dat nigger man done gone!"

"Don't you think you did wrong to hit him?" Miss Tewksbury asked.

"Dat w'at Miss 'Ria say. She say I oughter be shame er myse'f by good rights; but w'at dat nigger man wanter come hurtin' my feelin' fer w'en I settin' dar studyin' my lesson des hard ez I kin, right spang out'n de book? en spozen she wuz upper-side down, wa'n't de lesson in dar all de time, kaze how she gwine spill out?"

William was very serious — indeed, he was indignant — when he closed his argument. He turned to go out, but paused at the door, and said, —

"Miss 'Ria say supper be ready 'mos' 'fo' you kin turn 'roun', but she say ef you too tired out she'll have it sont up." William paused, rolled his eyes towards the ceiling, smacked his mouth, and added, "I gwine fetch in de batter-cakes myse'f."

Miss Tewksbury felt in her soul that she ought to be horrified at this recital; but she was grateful that she was not amused.

"Aunt Harriet," cried Helen, when William had disappeared, "this is better than the seashore. I am stronger already. My only regret is that Henry P. Bassett, the novelist, is not here. The last time I saw him, he was moping and complaining that his occupation was almost gone, because he had exhausted all the types — that's what he calls them. He declared he would be compelled to take his old characters, and give them a new outfit of emotions. Oh, if he were only here!"

"I hope you feel that you are, in some sense, responsible for all this, Helen," said Miss Tewksbury solemnly.

"Do you mean the journey, aunt Harriet, or the little negro?"

"My dear child, don't pretend to misunderstand me. I cannot help feeling that if we had done and were doing our whole duty, this — this poor negro — Ah, well! it is useless to speak of it. We are on missionary ground, but our hands are tied. Oh, I wish Elizabeth Mappis were here! She would teach us our duty."

"She wouldn't teach me mine, Aunt Harriet," said Helen seriously. "I wouldn't give one grain of your common-sense for all that Elizabeth Mappis has written and spoken. What have her wild theories to do with these people? She acts like a man in disguise. When I see her striding about, delivering her harangues, I always imagine she is wearing a pair of cowhide boots as a sort of stimulus to her masculinity. Ugh! I'm glad she isn't here."

Ordinarily, Miss Tewksbury would have defended Mrs. Elizabeth Mappis; but she remembered that a defence of that remarkable woman — as remarkable for her intellect as for her courage — was unnecessary at all times, and, in this instance, absolutely uncalled for. Moreover, the clangor of the supper-bell, which rang out at that moment, would have effectually drowned out whatever Miss Tewksbury might have chosen to say in behalf of Mrs. Mappis.

The bellringer was William, the genial little negro whose acquaintance the ladies had made, and he performed his duty with an unction that left nothing to be desired. The bell was so large that William was compelled to use both hands in swinging it. He bore it from the dining-room to the hall, and thence from one veranda to the other, making fuss enough to convince everybody that those who ate at the tavern were on the point of enjoying another of the famous meals prepared under the supervision of Mrs. Haley.

There was nothing in the dining-room to invite the criticism of Helen and her aunt, even though

they had been disposed to be critical; there was no
evidence of slatternly management. Every thing was
plain, but neat. The ceiling was high and wide;
and the walls were of dainty whiteness, relieved
here and there by bracket-shelves containing shiny
crockery and glass-ware. The oil-lamps gave a
mellow light through the simple but unique paper
shades with which they had been fitted. Above the
table, which extended the length of the room, was
suspended a series of large fans. These fans were
connected by a cord, so that when it became necessary to cool the room, or to drive away the flies, one
small negro, by pulling a string, could set them all
in motion.

Over this dining-room Mrs. Haley presided. She
sat at the head of the table, serene, cheerful, and
watchful, anticipating the wants of each and every
one who ate at the board. She invited Helen and
her aunt to seats near her own, and somehow managed to convince them, veteran travellers though
they were, that hospitality such as hers was richly
worth paying for.

"I do hope you'll make out to be comfortable in
this poor little neighborhood," she said as the ladies
lingered over their tea, after the other boarders —
the clerks and the shopkeepers — had bolted their
food and fare. "I have my hopes, and I have my
doubts. Gener'l Garwood says you're come to mend
your health," she continued, regarding the ladies

with the critical eye of one who has had something to do with herbs and simples; "and I've been tryin' my best to pick out which is the sick one, but it's a mighty hard matter. Yet I won't go by looks, because if folks looked bad every time they felt bad, they'd be some mighty peaked people in this world off and on. — William, run and fetch in some hot batter-cakes."

"I am the alleged invalid," said Helen. "I am the victim of a conspiracy between my aunt here and our family physician. — Aunt Harriet, what do you suppose Dr. Buxton would say if he knew how comfortable we are at this moment? I dare say he would write a letter, and order us off to some other point."

"My niece," said Miss Tewksbury, by way of explanation, "has weak lungs, but she has never permitted herself to acknowledge the fact."

"Well, my goodness!" exclaimed Mrs. Haley, "if that's all, we'll have her sound and well in a little or no time. Why, when I was her age I had a hackin' cough and a rackin' pain in my breast night and day, and I fell off till my own blood kin didn't know me. Everybody give me up; but old Miss Polly Flanders in Hancock, right j'inin' county from Greene, she sent me word to make me some mullein-tea, and drink sweet milk right fresh from the cow; and from that day to this I've never know'd what weak lungs was. I reckon you'll be mighty lonesome here," said

Mrs. Haley, after William had returned with a fresh supply of batter-cakes, " but you'll find folks mighty neighborly, once you come to know 'em. And, bless goodness, here's one of 'em now! — Howdy, Emma Jane?"

A tall, ungainly-looking woman stood in the door of the dining-room leading to the kitchen. Her appearance showed the most abject poverty. Her dirty sunbonnet had fallen back from her head, and hung on her shoulders. Her hair was of a reddish-gray color, and its frazzled and tangled condition suggested that the woman had recently passed through a period of extreme excitement; but this suggestion was promptly corrected by the wonderful serenity of her face, — a pale, unhealthy-looking face, with sunken eyes, high cheek-bones, and thin lips that seemed never to have troubled themselves to smile : a burnt-out face that had apparently surrendered to the past, and had no hope for the future. The Puritan simplicity of the woman's dress made her seem taller than she really was, but this was the only illusion about her. Though her appearance was uncouth and ungainly, her manner was unembarrassed. She looked at Helen with some degree of interest ; and to the latter it seemed that Misery, hopeless but unabashed, gazed at her with a significance at once pathetic and appalling. In response to Mrs. Haley's salutation, the woman seated herself in the doorway, and sighed.

"You must be tired, Emma Jane, not to say howdy," said Mrs. Haley, with a smile. The woman raised her right hand above her head, and allowed it to drop helplessly into her lap.

"Ti-ud! Lordy, Lordy! how kin a pore creetur' like me be ti-ud? Hain't I thes natally made out'n i'on?"

"Well, I won't go so fur as to say that, Emma Jane," said Mrs. Haley, "but you're mighty tough. Now, you know that yourself."

"Yes'n — yes'n. I'm made out'n i'on. Lordy, Lordy! I thes natally hone fer some un ter come along an' tell me what makes me h'ist up an' walk away over yan' ter the railroad track, an' set thar tell the ingine shoves by. I wisht some un ud up an' tell me what makes me so restless an' oneasy, ef it hain't 'cause I'm hungry. I thes wisht they would. Passin' on by, I sez ter myself, s' I, 'Emma Jane Stucky,' s' I, 'ef you know what's good fer your wholesome,' s' I, 'you'll sneak in on Miss Haley, 'cause you'll feel better,' s' I, 'ef you don't no more'n tell 'er howdy,' s' I. Lordy, Lordy! I dunner what ud 'come er me ef I hadn't a bin made out'n i'on."

"Emma Jane," said Mrs. Haley, in the tone of one who is humoring a child, "these ladies are from the North."

"Yes'n," said the woman, glancing at Helen and her aunt with the faintest expression of pity; "yes'n, I hearn tell you had comp'ny. Hit's a mighty long

ways fum this, the North, hain't it, Miss Haley, —
a long ways fuder'n Tennissy? Well, the Lord
knows I pity um fum the bottom of my heart, that I
do — a-bein' such a long ways fum home."

"The North is ever so much farther than Tennessee," said Helen pleasantly, almost unconsciously
assuming the tone employed by Mrs. Haley; "but
the weather is so very cold there that we have to
run away sometimes."

"You're right, honey," said Mrs. Stucky, hugging
herself with her long arms. "I wisht I could run
away fum it myself. Ef I wa'n't made out'n i'on, I
dunner how I'd stan' it. Lordy! when the win' sets
in from the east, hit in-about runs me plum de-
stracted. Hit kills lots an' lots er folks, but they
hain't made out'n i'on like me."

While Mrs. Stucky was describing the vigorous
constitution that had enabled her to survive in the
face of various difficulties, and in spite of many mis-
haps, Mrs. Haley was engaged in making up a little
parcel of victuals. This she handed to the woman.

"Thanky-do! thanky-do, ma'am! Me an' my son'll
set down an' wallop this up, an' say thanky-do all the
time, an' atter we're done we'll wipe our mouves, an'
say thanky-do."

"I reckon you ladies'll think we're mighty queer
folks down here," said Mrs. Haley, with an air of
apology, after Mrs. Stucky had retired; "but I declare I can't find it in my heart to treat that poor

creetur' out of the way. I set and look at her sometimes, and I wish I may never budge if I don't come
mighty nigh cryin'. She ain't hardly fittin' to live,
and if she's fittin' to die, she's lots better off than the
common run of folks. But she's mighty worrysome.
She pesters me lots mor'n I ever let on."

"The poor creature!" exclaimed Miss Tewksbury.
"I am truly sorry for her — truly sorry."

"Ah! so am I," said Helen. "I propose to see
more of her. I am interested in just such people."

"Well, ma'am," said Mrs. Haley dryly, "if you
like sech folks it's a thousand pities you've come
here, for you'll git a doste of 'em. Yes'm, that you
will; a doste of 'em that'll last you as long as you
live, if you live to be one of the patrioks. And
you nee'nter be sorry for Emma Jane Stucky neither.
Jest as you see her now, jesso she's been a-goin' on
fer twenty year, an' jest as you see her now, jesso
she's been a-lookin' ev'ry sence anybody around here
has been a-knowin' her."

"Her history must be a pathetic one," said Miss
Tewksbury with a sigh.

"Her what, ma'am?" asked Mrs. Haley.

"Her history, the story of her life," responded
Miss Tewksbury. "I dare say it is very touching."

"Well, ma'am," said Mrs. Haley, "Emma Jane
Stucky is like one of them there dead pines out
there in the clearin'. If you had a stack of almanacs
as high as a hoss-rack, you couldn't pick out the

—year she was young and sappy. She must 'a' started
out as a light'd knot, an' she's been a-gittin' tougher
year in an' year out, till now she's tougher'n the
toughest. No'm," continued Mrs. Haley, replying
to an imaginary argument, " I ain't predijiced agin
the poor creetur' — the Lord knows I ain't. If I
was, no vittels would she git from me, — not a
scrimption."

"I never saw such an expression on a human
countenance," said Helen. " Her eyes will haunt
me as long as I live."

"Bless your soul and body, child !" exclaimed
Mrs. Haley ; " if you're going to let that poor creetur's looks pester you, you'll be worried to death, as
certain as the world. There's a hunderd in this
settlement jest like her, and ther' must be more'n
that, old an' young, 'cause the children look to be
as old as the'r grannies. I reckon maybe you ain't
used to seein' piney-woods Tackies. Well, ma'am,
you wait till you come to know 'em, and if you are
in the habits of bein' ha'nted by looks, you'll be the
wuss ha'nted mortal in this land, 'less'n it's them
that's got the sperrit-rappin's after 'em."

IV.

Mrs. Stucky, making her way homeward through
the gathering dusk, moved as noiselessly and as
swiftly as a ghost. The soft white sand beneath her

feet gave forth no sound, and she seemed to be glid-
ing forward, rather than walking; though there was
a certain awkward emphasis and decision in her
movements altogether human in their suggestions.
The way was lonely. There was no companionship
for her in the whispering sighs of the tall pines that
stood by the roadside, no friendliness in the constellations that burned and sparkled overhead, no hospitable suggestion in the lights that gleamed faintly
here and there from the windows of the houses in
the little settlement. To Mrs. Stucky all was commonplace. There was nothing in her surroundings
as she went towards her home, to lend wings even
to her superstition, which was eager to assert itself
on all occasions.

It was not much of a home to which she was making her way, — a little log-cabin in a pine thicket, surrounded by a little clearing that served to show how
aimlessly and how hopelessly the lack of thrift and
energy could assert itself. The surroundings were
mean enough and squalid enough at their best, but
the oppressive shadows of night made them meaner
and more squalid than they really were. The sun,
which shines so lavishly in that region, appeared to
glorify the squalor, showing wild passion-flowers
clambering along the broken-down fence of pine-
poles, and a wisteria vine running helter-skelter
across the roof of the little cabin. But the night
hid all this completely.

A dim, vague blaze, springing from a few charred pine-knots, made the darkness visible in the one room of the cabin; and before it, with his elbows on his knees and his chin in his hands, sat what appeared to be a man. He wore neither coat nor shoes, and his hair was long and shaggy.

"Is that you, Bud?" said Mrs. Stucky.

"Why, who'd you reckon it wuz, maw?" replied Bud, looking up with a broad grin that was not at all concealed by his thin sandy beard. "A body'd sorter think, ef they 'uz ter ketch you gwine on that away, that you 'spected ter find some great somebody er nuther a-roostin' in here."

Mrs. Stucky, by way of responding, stirred the pine-knots until they gave forth a more satisfactory light, hung her bonnet on the bedpost, and seated herself wearily in a rickety chair, the loose planks of the floor rattling and shaking as she moved about.

"Now, who in the nation did you reckon it wuz, maw?" persisted Bud, still grinning placidly.

"Some great somebody," replied Mrs. Stucky, brushing her gray hair out of her eyes and looking at her son. At this, Bud could contain himself no longer. He laughed almost uproariously.

"Well, the great Jemimy!" he exclaimed, and then laughed louder than ever.

"Wher've you been?" Mrs. Stucky asked, when Bud's mirth had subsided.

"Away over yander at the depot," said Bud,

indicating Little Azalia. "An' I fotch you some May-pops too. I did that! I seed 'em while I wuz a-gwine 'long, an' I sez ter myself, sezee, 'You jess wait thar tell I come 'long back, an' I'll take an' take you ter maw,' sezee."

Although this fruit of the passion-flower was growing in profusion right at the door, Mrs. Stucky gave this grown man, her son, to understand that May-pops such as he brought were very desirable indeed.

"I wonder you didn't fergit 'em," she said.

"Who? me!" exclaimed Bud. "I jess like fer ter see anybody ketch me fergittin' 'em. Now I jess would. I never eat a one, nuther — not a one."

Mrs. Stucky made no response to this, and none seemed to be necessary. Bud sat and pulled his thin beard, and gazed in the fire. Presently he laughed and said, —

"I jess bet a hoss you couldn't guess who I seed; now I jess bet that."

Mrs. Stucky rubbed the side of her face thought-fully, and seemed to be making a tremendous effort to imagine whom Bud had seen.

"'Twer'n't no man, en 'twer'n't no Azalia folks. 'Twuz a gal."

"A gal!" exclaimed Mrs. Stucky.

"Yes'n, a gal, an' *ef* she wa'n't a zooner you may jess take an' knock my chunk out."

Mrs. Stucky looked at her son curiously. Her cold gray eyes glittered in the firelight as she held

them steadily on his face. Bud, conscious of this
inspection, moved about in his chair uneasily, shift-
ing his feet from one side to the other.

"'Twer'n't no Sal Badger," he said, after a while,
laughing sheepishly; "'twer'n't no Maria Matthews,
'twer'n't no Lou Hornsby, an' 'twer'n't no Martha
Jane Williams, nuther. She wuz a bran'-new gal,
an' she went ter the tavern, *she* did."

"I've done saw 'er," said Mrs. Stucky placidly.

"You done saw 'er, maw!" exclaimed Bud. "Well,
the great Jemimy! What's her name, maw?"

"They didn't call no names," said Mrs. Stucky.
"They jess sot thar, an' gormandized on waffles an'
batter-cakes, an' didn't call no names. Hit made
me dribble at the mouf, the way they went on."

"Wuz she purty, maw?"

"I sot an' looked at um," Mrs. Stucky went on,
"an' I 'lowed maybe the war moughter come betwixt
the old un an' her good looks. The t'other one
looks mighty slick, but, Lordy! She hain't nigh ez
slick ez that ar Lou Hornsby; yit she's got lots
purtier motions."

"Well, I seed 'er, maw," said Bud, gazing into
the depths of the fireplace. "Atter the ingine come
a-snortin' by, I jumped up behind the hack whar they
puts the trunks, an' I got a right good glimp' un 'er;
an' ef she hain't purty, then I dunner what purty is.
What'd you say her name wuz, maw?"

"Lordy, jess hark ter the creetur! Hain't I jess

this minute hollered, an' tole you that they hain't
called no names?"

"I 'lowed maybe you moughter hearn the name
named, an' then drapt it," said Bud, still gazing into
the fire. "I tell you what, she made that ole hack
look big, *she* did!"

"You talk like you er start crazy, Bud!" exclaimed
Mrs. Stucky, leaning over, and fixing her glittering
eyes on his face. "Lordy! what's she by the side
er me? Is she made out'n i'on?"

Bud's enthusiasm immediately vanished, and a
weak, flickering smile took possession of his face.

"No'm — no'm; that she hain't made out'n i'on!
She's lots littler'n you is — lots littler. She looks
like she's sorry."

"Sorry! What fer?"

"Sorry fer we-all."

Mrs. Stucky looked at her son with amazement,
not unmixed with indignation. Then she seemed to
remember something she had forgotten.

"Sorry fer we-all, honey, when we er got this
great big pile er tavern vittles?" she asked with a
smile; and then the two fell to, and made the most
of Mrs. Haley's charity.

At the tavern Helen and her aunt sat long at
their tea, listening to the quaint gossip of Mrs.
Haley, which not only took a wide and entertaining
range, but entered into details that her guests found
extremely interesting. Miss Tewksbury's name re-

minded Mrs. Haley of a Miss Kingsbury, a Northern lady, who had taught school in Middle Georgia, and who had "writ a sure-enough book," as the genial landlady expressed it. She went to the trouble of hunting up this " sure-enough " book, — a small school dictionary, — and gave many reminiscences of her acquaintance with the author.

In the small parlor, too, the ladies found Gen. Garwood awaiting them ; and they held quite a little reception, forming the acquaintance, among others, of Miss Lou Hornsby, a fresh-looking young woman, who had an exclamation of surprise or a grimace of wonder for every statement she heard and for every remark that was made. Miss Hornsby also went to the piano, and played and sang "Nelly Gray" and "Lily Dale" with a dramatic fervor that could only have been acquired in a boarding-school. The Rev. Arthur Hill was also there, a little gentleman, whose side-whiskers and modest deportment betokened both refinement and sensibility. He was very cordial to the two ladies from the North, and strove to demonstrate the liberality of his cloth by a certain gayety of manner that was by no means displeasing. He seemed to consider himself one of the links of sociability, as well as master of ceremonies ; and he had a way of speaking for others that suggested considerable social tact and versatility. Thus, when there was a lull in the conversation, he started it again, and imparted to it a vivacity that was certainly

remarkable, as Helen thought. At precisely the
proper moment, he seized Miss Hornsby, and bore
her off home, tittering sweetly as only a young girl
can ; and the others, following the example thus
happily set, left Helen and her aunt to themselves,
and to the repose that tired travellers are supposed
to be in need of. They were not long in seeking it.

"I wonder," said Helen, after she and her aunt
had gone to bed, "if these people really regard us
as enemies?"

This question caused Miss Tewksbury to sniff the
air angrily.

"Pray, what difference does it make?" she replied.

"Oh, none at all!" said Helen. "I was just
thinking. The little preacher was tremendously
gay. His mind seemed to be on skates. He touched
on every subject but the war, and that he glided
around gracefully. No doubt they have had enough
of war down here."

"I should hope so," said Miss Tewksbury. "Go
to sleep, child : you need rest."

Helen did not follow this timely advice at once.
From her window she could see the constellations
dragging their glittering procession westward ; and
she knew that the spirit of the night was whispering gently in the tall pines, but her thoughts were
in a whirl. The scenes through which she had
passed, and the people she had met, were new to
her ; and she lay awake and thought of them until

at last the slow-moving stars left her wrapped in sleep, — a sleep from which she was not aroused until William shook the foundations of the tavern with his melodious bell, informing everybody that the hour for breakfast had arrived.

Shortly afterwards, William made his appearance in person, bringing an abundance of fresh, clear water. He appeared to be in excellent humor.

"What did you say your name is?" Helen asked. William chuckled, as if he thought the question was in the nature of a joke.

"I'm name' Willum, ma'm, en my mammy she name' Sa'er Jane, en de baby she name' Phillypeener. Miss 'Ria she say dat baby is de likelies' nigger baby w'at she y'ever been see sence de war, en I speck she is, kaze Miss 'Ria ain't been talk dat away 'bout eve'y nigger baby w'at come 'long."

"How old are you?" Miss Tewksbury inquired.

"I dunno'm," said William placidly. "Miss 'Ria she says I'm lots older dan w'at I looks ter be, en I speck dat's so, kaze mammy say dey got ter be a runt 'mongst all folks's famblies."

Helen laughed, and William went on : —

"Mammy say ole Miss gwine come see you all. Mars Peyt gwine bring 'er."

"Who is old Miss?" Helen asked.

William gazed at her with unfeigned amusement.

"Dunner who ole Miss is? Lordy! you de fus' folks w'at ain't know ole Miss. She Mars Peyt's own mammy, dat's who she is, en ef she come lak dey say she comin', hit'll be de fus' time she y'ever sot foot in dish yer tavern less'n 'twuz indurance er de war. Miss 'Ria say she wish ter goodness ole Miss 'ud sen' word ef she gwine stay ter dinner so she kin fix up somepin n'er nice. I dunno whe'er Miss Hallie comin' er no, but ole Miss comin', sho, kaze I done been year um sesso."

"And who is Miss Hallie?" Helen inquired, as William still lingered.

"Miss Hallie — she — dunno'm, ceppin' she des stays dar 'long wid um. Miss 'Ria say she mighty quare, but I wish turrer folks wuz quare lak Miss Hallie."

William staid until he was called away, and at breakfast Mrs. Haley imparted the information which, in William's lingo, had sounded somewhat scrappy. It was to the effect that Gen. Garwood's mother would call on the ladies during their stay. Mrs. Haley laid great stress on the statement.

"Such an event seems to be very interesting," Helen said rather dryly.

"Yes'm," said Mrs. Haley, with her peculiar emphasis, "it ruther took me back when I heard the niggers talkin' about it this mornin'. If that old lady has ever darkened my door, I've done forgot it. She's mighty nice and neighborly," Mrs. Haley went on, in response to a smile which Helen gave her aunt, "but she don't go out much. Oh, she's nice and proud; Lord, if pride 'ud kill a body, that old 'oman would 'a' been dead too long ago to talk about. They're all proud — the whole kit and b'ilin'. She mayn't be too proud to come to this here tavern, but I know she ain't never been here. The preacher used to say that pride drives out grace, but I don't believe it, because that 'ud strip the Garwoods of all they've got in this world; and I know they're just as good as they can be."

"I heard the little negro boy talking of Miss Hallie," said Helen. "Pray, who is she?"

Mrs. Haley closed her eyes, threw her head back, and laughed softly.

"The poor child!" she exclaimed. "I declare, I feel like cryin' every time I think about her. She's the forlornest poor creetur the Lord ever let live, and one of the best. Sometimes, when I git tore up in my mind, and begin to think that every thing's wrong-end foremost, I jess think of Hallie Garwood, and then I don't have no more trouble."

Both Helen and her aunt appeared to be interested, and Mrs. Haley went on : —

"The poor child was a Herndon; I reckon you've heard tell of the Virginia Herndons. At the beginning of the war, she was married to Ethel Garwood; and, bless your life, she hadn't been married more'n a week before Ethel was killed. 'Twa'n't in no battle, but jess in a kind of skirmish. They fotch him home, and Hallie come along with him, and right

here she's been ev'ry sence.   She does mighty quare.
She don't wear nothin' but black, and she don't go
nowhere less'n it's somewheres where there's sickness.   It makes my blood run cold to think about
that poor creetur.   Trouble hits some folks and
glances off, and it hits some and thar it sticks.   I
tell you what, them that it gives the go-by ought to
be monst'ous proud."

This was the beginning of many interesting experiences for Helen and her aunt.   They managed
to find considerable comfort in Mrs. Haley's genial
gossip.   It amused and instructed them, and, at the
same time, gave them a standard, half-serious, half-
comical, by which to measure their own experiences
in what seemed to them a very quaint neighborhood.
They managed, in the course of a very few days, to
make themselves thoroughly at home in their new
surroundings ; and, while they missed much that
tradition and literature had told them they would
find, they found much to excite their curiosity and
attract their interest.

One morning, an old-fashioned carriage, drawn by
a pair of heavy-limbed horses, lumbered up to the
tavern door.   Helen watched it with some degree
of expectancy.   The curtains and upholstering were
faded and worn, and the panels were dingy with age.
The negro driver was old and obsequious.   He
jumped from his high seat, opened the door, let
down a flight of steps, and then stood with his

hat off, the November sun glistening on his bald
head. Two ladies alighted. One was old, and one
was young, but both were arrayed in deep mourning.
The old lady had an abundance of gray hair that
was combed straight back from her forehead, and
her features gave evidence of great decision of
character. The young lady had large, lustrous eyes,
and the pallor of her face was in strange contrast
with her sombre drapery. These were the ladies
from Waverly, as the Garwood place was called; and
Helen and her aunt met them a few moments later.

"I am so pleased to meet you," said the old lady,
with a smile that made her face beautiful. "And
this is Miss Tewksbury. Really, I have heard my
son speak of you so often that I seem to know you.
This is my daughter Hallie. She doesn't go out
often, but she insisted on coming with me to-day."

"I'm very glad you came," said Helen, sitting by
the pale young woman after the greetings were
over.

"I think you are lovely," said Hallie, with the
tone of one who is settling a question that had previously been debated. Her clear eyes from which
innocence, unconquered and undimmed by trouble,
shone forth, fastened themselves on Helen's face.
The admiration they expressed was unqualified and
unadulterated. It was the admiration of a child.
But the eyes were not those of a child: they were
such as Helen had seen in old paintings, and the

pathos that seemed part of their beauty belonged
definitely to the past.

"I lovely?" exclaimed Helen in astonishment,
blushing a little. "I have never been accused of
such a thing before."

"You have such a beautiful complexion," Hallie
went on placidly, her eyes still fixed on Helen's face.
"I had heard — some one had told me — that you
were an invalid. I was so sorry." The beautiful
eyes drooped, and Hallie sighed gently.

"My invalidism is a myth," Helen replied, somewhat puzzled to account for the impression the pale
young woman made on her. "It is the invention of
my aunt and our family physician. They have a
theory that my lungs are affected, and that the air
of the pine-woods will do me good."

"Oh, I hope and trust it will," exclaimed Hallie,
with an earnestness that Helen could trace to no
reasonable basis but affectation. "Oh, I do hope it
will! You are so young — so full of life."

"My dear child," said Helen, with mock gravity,
"I am older than you are, — ever so much older."

The lustrous eyes closed, and for a moment the long
silken lashes rested against the pale cheek. Then
the eyes opened, and gazed at Helen appealingly.

"Oh, impossible! How could that be? I was
sixteen in 1862."

"Then," said Helen, "you are twenty-seven, and
I am twenty-five."

"I knew it, — I felt it!" exclaimed Hallie, with pensive animation.

Helen was amused and somewhat interested. She admired the peculiar beauty of Hallie; but the efforts of the latter to repress her feelings, to reach, as it were, the results of self-effacement, were not at all pleasing to the Boston girl.

Mrs. Garwood and Miss Tewksbury found themselves on good terms at once. A course of novel-reading, seasoned with reflection, had led Miss Tewksbury to believe that Southern ladies of the first families possessed in a large degree the Oriental faculty of laziness. She had pictured them in her mind as languid creatures, with a retinue of servants to carry their smelling-salts, and to stir the tropical air with palm-leaf fans. Miss Tewksbury was pleased rather than disappointed to find that Mrs. Garwood did not realize her idea of a Southern woman. The large, lumbering carriage was something, and the antiquated driver threatened to lead the mind in a somewhat romantic direction; but both were shabby enough to be regarded as relics and reminders rather than as active possibilities.

Mrs. Garwood was bright and cordial, and the air of refinement about her was pronounced and unmistakable. Miss Tewksbury told her that Dr. Buxton had recommended Azalia as a sanitarium.

"Ephraim Buxton!" exclaimed Mrs. Garwood. "Why, you don't tell me that Ephraim Buxton is practising medicine in Boston? And do you really know him? Why, Ephraim Buxton was my first sweetheart!"

Mrs. Garwood's laugh was pleasant to hear, and her blushes were worth looking at as she referred to Dr. Buxton. Miss Tewksbury laughed sympathetically but primly.

"It was quite romantic," Mrs. Garwood went on, in a half-humorous, half-confidential tone. "Ephraim was the school-teacher here, and I was his eldest scholar. He was young and green and awkward, but the best-hearted, the most generous mortal I ever saw. I made quite a hero of him."

"Well," said Miss Tewksbury, in her matter-of-fact way, "I have never seen any thing very heroic about Dr. Buxton. He comes and goes, and prescribes his pills, like all other doctors."

"Ah, that was forty years ago," said Mrs. Garwood, laughing. "A hero can become very commonplace in forty years. Dr. Buxton must be a dear good man. Is he married?"

"No," said Miss Tewksbury. "He has been wise in his day and generation."

"What a pity!" exclaimed the other. "He would have made some woman happy."

Mrs. Garwood asked many questions concerning the physician who had once taught school at Azalia; and the conversation of the two ladies finally took a range that covered all New England, and, finally,

the South. Each was surprised at the remarkable
ignorance of the other; but their ignorance covered
different fields, so that they had merely to exchange
facts and information and experiences in order to
entertain each other. They touched on the war deli-
cately, though Miss Tewksbury had never cultivated
the art of reserve to any great extent. At the same
time there was no lack of frankness on either side.

"My son has been telling me of some of the little
controversies he had with you," said Mrs. Garwood.
"He says you fairly bristle with arguments."

"The general never heard half my arguments,"
replied Miss Tewksbury. "He never gave me an
opportunity to use them."

"My son is very conservative," said Mrs. Garwood,
with a smile in which could be detected a mother's
fond pride. "After the war he felt the responsibility
of his position. A great many people looked up to
him. For a long time after the surrender we had
no law and no courts, and there was a great deal of
confusion. Oh, you can't imagine! Every man was
his own judge and jury."

"So I've been told," said Miss Tewksbury.

"Of course you know something about it, but you
can have no conception of the real condition of
things. It was a tremendous upheaval coming after
a terrible struggle, and my son felt that some one
should set an example of prudence. His theory was,
and is, that every thing was for the best, and that

our people should make the best of it. I think he was right," Mrs. Garwood added with a sigh, "but I don't know."

"Why, unquestionably!" exclaimed Miss Tewksbury. She was going on to say more ; she felt that here was an opening for some of her arguments : but her eyes fell on Hallie, whose pale face and sombre garb formed a curious contrast to the fresh-looking young woman who sat beside her. Miss Tewksbury paused.

"Did you lose any one in the war?" Hallie was asking softly.

"I lost a darling brother," Helen replied.

Hallie laid her hand on Helen's arm, a beautiful white hand. The movement was at once a gesture and a caress.

"Dear heart!" she said, "you must come and see me. We will talk together. I love those who are sorrowful."

Miss Tewksbury postponed her arguments, and after some conversation the visitors took their leave.

"Aunt Harriet," said Helen, when they were alone, "what do you make of these people? Did you see that poor girl, and hear her talk? She chilled me and entranced me."

"Don't talk so, child," said Miss Tewksbury; "they are very good people, much better people than I thought we should find in this wilderness. It is a comfort to talk to them."

"But that poor girl," said Helen. "She is a mystery to me. She reminds me of a figure I have seen on the stage, or read about in some old book."

When Azalia heard that the Northern ladies had been called on by the mistress of Waverly, that portion of its inhabitants which was in the habit of keeping up the forms of sociability made haste to follow her example, so that Helen and her aunt were made to feel at home in spite of themselves. Gen. Garwood was a frequent caller, ostensibly to engage in sectional controversies with Miss Tewksbury, which he seemed to enjoy keenly; but Mrs. Haley observed that when Helen was not visible the general rarely prolonged his discussions with her aunt.

The Rev. Arthur Hill also called with some degree of regularity; and it was finally understood that Helen would, at least temporarily, take the place of Miss Lou Hornsby as organist of the little Episcopal church in the Tackey settlement, as soon as Mr. Goolsby, the fat and enterprising book-agent, had led the fair Louisa to the altar. This wedding occurred in due time, and was quite an event in Azalia's social history. Goolsby was stout, but gallant; and Miss Hornsby made a tolerably handsome bride, notwithstanding a tendency to giggle when her deportment should have been dignified. Helen furnished the music, Gen. Garwood gave the bride away, and the little preacher read the ceremony quite impressively; so that with the flowers and other favors, and the subsequent dinner, — which Mrs. Haley called an "infair," — the occasion was a very happy and successful one.

Among those who were present, not as invited guests, but by virtue of their unimportance, were Mrs. Stucky and her son Bud. They were followed and flanked by quite a number of their neighbors, who gazed on the festal scene with an impressive curiosity that cannot be described. Pale-faced, wide-eyed, statuesque, their presence, interpreted by a vivid imagination, might have been regarded as an omen of impending misfortune. They stood on the outskirts of the wedding company, gazing on the scene apparently without an emotion of sympathy or interest. They were there, it seemed, to see what new caper the townspeople had concluded to cut, to regard it solemnly, and to regret it with grave faces when the lights were out and the fantastic procession had drifted away to the village.

The organ in the little church was a fine instrument, though a small one. It had belonged to the little preacher's wife, and he had given it to the church. To his mind, the fact that she had used it sanctified it, and he had placed it in the church as a part of the sacrifice he felt called on to make in behalf of his religion. Helen played it with uncommon skill, — a skill born of a passionate appreciation of music in its highest forms. The Rev. Mr. Hill listened like one entranced, but Helen

played unconscious of his admiration. On the outskirts of the congregation she observed Mrs. Stucky,
and by her side a young man with long sandy hair,
evidently uncombed, and a thin stubble of beard.
Helen saw this young man pull Mrs. Stucky by
the sleeve, and direct her attention to the organ.
Instead of looking in Helen's direction, Mrs. Stucky
fixed her eyes on the face of the young man and
held them there; but he continued to stare at
the organist. It was a gaze at once mournful and
appealing, — not different in that respect from
the gaze of any of the queer people around him,
but it affected Miss Eustis strangely. To her quick
imagination, it suggested loneliness, despair, that
was the more tragic because of its isolation. It
seemed to embody the mute, pent-up distress of
whole generations. Somehow Helen felt herself to
be playing for the benefit of this poor creature. The
echoes of the wedding-march sounded grandly in the
little church, then came a softly played interlude,
and finally a solemn benediction, in which solicitude
seemed to be giving happiness a sweet warning. As
the congregation filed out of the church, the organ
sent its sonorous echoes after the departing crowd,
— echoes that were taken up by the whispering and
sighing pines, and borne far into the night.

Mrs. Stucky did not go until after the lights were
out; and then she took her son by the hand, and the
two went to their lonely cabin not far away. They

went in, and soon had a fire kindled on the hearth.
No word had passed between them; but after a
while, when Mrs. Stucky had taken a seat in the
corner, and lit her pipe, she exclaimed, —

"Lordy! what a great big gob of a man! I dunner
what on the face er the yeth Lou Hornsby could 'a'
been a-dreamin' about. From the way she's been
a-gigglin' aroun' I'd 'a' thought she'd 'a' sot her cap
fer the giner'l."

"I say it!" said Bud, laughing loudly. "Whatter
you reckon the giner'l 'ud 'a' been a-doin' all that
time? I see 'er now, a-gigglin' an' a-settin' 'er cap
fer the giner'l. Lordy, yes!"

"What's the matter betwixt you an' Lou?" asked
Mrs. Stucky grimly. "'Tain't been no time senst
you wuz a-totin' water fer her ma, an' a-hangin'
aroun' whilst she played the music in the church
thar." Bud continued to laugh. "But, Lordy!"
his mother went on, "I reckon you'll be a-totin'
water an' a-runnin' er'n's fer thish yer Yankee gal
what played on the orgin up thar jess now."

"Well, they hain't no tellin'," said Bud, rubbing
his thin beard reflectively. "She's mighty spry
'long er that orgin, an' she's got mighty purty han's
an' mighty nimble fingers, an' ef she 'uz ter let down
her ha'r, she'd be plum ready ter fly."

"She walked home wi' the giner'l," said Mrs.
Stucky.

"I seed 'er," said Bud. "He sent some yuther

gals home in the carriage, an' him an' the Yankee
gal went a-walkin down the road. He humped up
his arm this away, an' the gal tuck it, an' off they
put." Bud seemed to enjoy the recollection of the
scene ; for he repeated, after waiting a while to see
what his mother would have to say, — " Yes, siree !
she tuck it, an' off they put."

Mrs. Stucky looked at this grown man, her son,
for a long time without saying any thing, and finally
remarked with something very like a sigh, —

" Well, honey, you neenter begrudge 'em the'r
walk. Hit's a long ways through the san'."

" Lordy, yes'n ! " exclaimed Bud with something
like a smile ; " it's a mighty long ways, but the giner'l
had the gal wi' 'im. He jess humped up his arm,
an' she tuck it, an' off they put."

It was even so. Gen. Garwood and Helen walked
home from the little church. The road was a long
but a shining one. In the moonlight the sand
shone white, save where little drifts and eddies
of pine-needles had gathered. But these were no
obstruction to the perspective, for the road was an
avenue, broad and level, that lost itself in the distance only because the companionable pines, inter-
lacing their boughs, contrived to present a background both vague and sombre, — a background that
receded on approach, and finally developed into the
village of Azalia and its suburbs.

Along this level and shining highway Helen and

Gen. Garwood went. The carriages that preceded them, and the people who walked with them or followed, gave a sort of processional pomp and movement to the gallant Goolsby's wedding, — so much so that if he could have witnessed it, his manly bosom would have swelled with genuine pride.

"The music you gave us was indeed a treat," said the general.

"It was perhaps more than you bargained for," Helen replied. "I suppose everybody thought I was trying to make a display, but I quite forgot myself. I was watching its effect on one of the poor creatures near the door — do you call them Tackies?"

"Yes, Tackies. Well, we are all obliged to the poor creature — man or woman. No doubt the fortunate person was Bud Stucky. I saw him standing near his mother. Bud is famous for his love of music. When the organ is to be played, Bud is always at the church; and sometimes he goes to Waverly, and makes Hallie play the piano for him while he sits out on the floor of the veranda near the window. Bud is quite a character."

"I am so sorry for him," said Helen gently.

"I doubt if he is to be greatly pitied," said the general. "Indeed, as the music was for him, and not for us, I think he is to be greatly envied."

"I see now," said Helen laughing, "that I should have restrained myself."

"The suggestion is almost selfish," said the general gallantly.

"Well, your nights here are finer than music," Helen remarked, fleeing to an impersonal theme. "To walk in the moonlight, without wraps and with no sense of discomfort, in the middle of December, is a wonderful experience to me. Last night I heard a mocking-bird singing; and my aunt has been asking Mrs. Haley if watermelons are ripe."

"The mocking-birds at Waverly," said the general, "have become something of a nuisance under Hallie's management. There is a great flock of them on the place, and in the summer they sing all night. It is not a very pleasant experience to have one whistling at your window the whole night through."

"Mrs. Haley," remarked Helen, "says that there are more mocking-birds now than there were before the war, and that they sing louder and more frequently."

"I shouldn't wonder," the general assented. "Mrs. Haley is quite an authority on such matters. Everybody quotes her opinions."

"I took the liberty the other day," Helen went on, "of asking her about the Ku Klux."

"And, pray, what did she say?" the general asked with some degree of curiosity.

"Why, she said they were like the shower of stars, — she had 'heard tell' of them, but she had never seen them. 'But,' said I, 'you have no doubt that the shower really occurred!'"

"Her illustration was somewhat unfortunate," the general remarked.

"Oh, by no means," Helen replied. "She looked at me with a twinkle in her eyes, and said she had heard that it wasn't the stars that fell, after all."

Talking thus, with long intervals of silence, the two walked along the gleaming road until they reached the tavern, where Miss Eustis found her aunt and Mrs. Haley waiting on the broad veranda.

"I don't think he is very polite," said Helen, after her escort had bade them good-night, and was out of hearing. "He offered me his arm, and then, after we had walked a little way, suggested that we could get along more comfortably by marching Indian file."

Mrs. Haley laughed loudly. "Why, bless your innocent heart, honey! that ain't nothin'. The sand's too deep in the road, and the path's too narrer for folks to be a-gwine along yarm-in-arm. Lord! don't talk about perliteness. That man's manners is somethin' better'n perliteness."

"Well," said Helen's aunt, "I can't imagine why he should want to make you trudge through the sand in that style."

"It is probably an output of the climate," said Helen.

"Well, now, honey," remarked Mrs. Haley, "if he ast you to walk wi' 'im, he had his reasons. I've got my own idee," she added with a chuckle. "I know one thing, — I know he's monstrous fond of some of the Northron folks. Ain't you never hearn, how, endurin' of the war, they fotch home a Yankee soldier along wi' Hallie's husband, an' buried 'em side by side? They tell me that Hallie's husband an' the Yankee was mighty nigh the same age, an' had a sorter favor. If that's so," said Mrs. Haley, with emphasis, "then two mighty likely chaps was knocked over on account of the everlastin' nigger."

All this was very interesting to Helen and her aunt, and they were anxious to learn all the particulars in regard to the young Federal soldier who had found burial at Waverly.

"What his name was," said Mrs. Haley, "I'll never tell you. Old Prince, the carriage-driver, can tell you lots more'n I can. He foun' 'em on the groun', an' he fotch 'em home. Prince use to be a mighty good nigger before freedom come out, but now he ain't much better'n the balance of 'em. You all 'ill see him when you go over thar, bekaze he's in an' out of the house constant. He'll tell you all about it if you're mighty perlite. Folks is got so they has to be mighty perlite to niggers sence the war. Yit I'll not deny that it's easy to be perlite to old Uncle Prince, bekaze he's mighty perlite hisself. He's what I call a high-bred nigger." Mrs. Haley said this with an air of pride, as if she were in some meas· ure responsible for Uncle Prince's good-breeding.

V.

IT came to pass that Helen Eustis and her aunt lost the sense of loneliness which they had found so oppressive during the first weeks of their visit. In the people about them they found a never-failing fund of entertainment. They found in the climate, too, a source of health and strength. The resinous odor of the pines was always in their nostrils; the far, faint undertones of music the winds made in the trees were always in their ears. The provinciality of the people, which some of the political correspondents describe as distressing, was so genuinely American in all its forms and manifestations, that these Boston women were enabled to draw from it, now and then, a whiff of New-England air. They recognized characteristics that made them feel thoroughly at home. Perhaps, so far as Helen was concerned, there were other reasons that reconciled her to her surroundings. At any rate, she was reconciled. More than this, she was happy. Her eyes sparkled, and the roses of health bloomed on her cheeks. All her movements were tributes to the buoyancy and energy of her nature. The little rector found out what this energy amounted to, when, on one occasion, he proposed to accompany her on one of her walks. It was a five-mile excursion; and he returned, as Mrs. Haley expressed it, "a used-up man."

One morning, just before Christmas, the Waverly carriage, driven in great state by Uncle Prince, drew up in front of the tavern; and in a few moments Helen and her aunt were given to understand that they had been sent for, in furtherance of an invitation they had accepted, to spend the holidays at Waverly.

"Ole Miss would 'a' come," said Uncle Prince, with a hospitable chuckle, "but she sorter ailin'; en Miss Hallie, she dat busy dat she ain't skacely got time fer ter tu'n 'roun'; so dey tuck'n sont atter you, ma'am, des like you wuz home folks."

The preparations of the ladies had already been made, and it was not long before they were swinging along under the green pines in the old-fashioned vehicle. Nor was it long before they passed from the pine forests, and entered the grove of live-oaks that shaded the walks and drives of Waverly. The house itself was a somewhat imposing structure, with a double veranda in front, supported by immense pillars, and surrounded on all sides by magnificent trees. Here, as Helen and her aunt had heard on all sides, a princely establishment had existed in the old time before the war, — an establishment noted for its lavish hospitality. Here visitors used to come in their carriages from all parts of Georgia, from South Carolina, and even from Virginia, — some of them remaining for weeks at a time, and giving to the otherwise dull neigh-

borhood long seasons of riotous festivity, which
were at once characteristic and picturesque. The
old days had gone to come no more, but there was
something in the atmosphere that seemed to recall
them. The stately yet simple architecture of the
house, the trees with their rugged and enormous
trunks, the vast extent of the grounds, — every
thing, indeed, that came under the eye, — seemed
to suggest the past. A blackened and broken
statue lay prone upon the ground hard by the
weather-beaten basin of a fountain long since dry.
Two tall granite columns, that once guarded an
immense gateway, supported the fragmentary skele-
tons of two colossal lamps. There was a suggestion not only of the old days before the war, but
of antiquity, — a suggestion that was intensified by
the great hall, the high ceilings, the wide fireplaces,
and the high mantels of the house itself. These
things somehow gave a weird aspect to Waverly in
the eyes of the visitors; but this feeling was largely
atoned for by the air of tranquillity that brooded
over the place, and it was utterly dispersed by the
heartiness with which they were welcomed.

"Here we is at home, ma'am," exclaimed Uncle
Prince, opening the carriage-door, and bowing low;
"en yon' come ole Miss en Miss Hallie."

The impression which Helen and her aunt received, and one which they never succeeded in
shaking off during their visit, was that they were

regarded as members of the family who had been away for a period, but who had now come home to stay. Just how these gentle hosts managed to impart this impression, Helen and Miss Tewksbury would have found it hard to explain; but they discovered that the art of entertaining was not a lost art even in the piney woods. Every incident, and even accidents, contributed to the enjoyment of the guests. Even the weather appeared to exert itself to please. Christmas morning was ushered in with a sharp little flurry of snow. The scene was a very pretty one, as the soft white flakes, some of them as large as a canary's wing, fell athwart the green foliage of the live-oaks and the magnolias.

"This is my hour!" exclaimed Helen enthusiastically.

"We enjoy it with you," said Hallie simply.

During the afternoon the clouds melted away, the sun came out, and the purple haze of Indian summer took possession of air and sky. In an hour the weather passed from the crisp and sparkling freshness of winter, to the wistful melancholy beauty of autumn.

"This," said Hallie gently, "is *my* hour." She was standing on the broad veranda with Helen. For reply, the latter placed her arm around the Southern girl; and they stood thus for a long time, their thoughts rhyming to the plaintive air of a negro melody that found its way across the fields and through the woods.

Christmas at Waverly, notwithstanding the fact that the negroes were free, was not greatly different from Christmas on the Southern plantations before the war. Few of the negroes who had been slaves had left the place, and those that remained knew how a Christmas ought to be celebrated. They sang the old-time songs, danced the old-time dances, and played the old-time plays.

All this was deeply interesting to the gentlewomen from Boston; but there was one incident that left a lasting impression on both, and probably had its effect in changing the future of one of them. It occurred one evening when they were all grouped around the fire in the drawing-room. The weather had grown somewhat colder than usual, and big hickory logs were piled in the wide fireplace. At the suggestion of Hallie the lights had been put out, and they sat in the ruddy glow of the firelight. The effect was picturesque indeed. The furniture and the polished wainscoting glinted and shone, and the shadows of the big brass andirons were thrown upon the ceiling, where they performed a witch's dance, the intricacy of which was amazing to behold.

It was an interesting group, representing the types of much that is best in the civilization of the two regions. Their talk covered a great variety of subjects, but finally drifted into reminiscences of the war, — reminiscences of its incidents rather than its passions.

"I have been told," said Miss Eustis, "that a dead

Union soldier was brought here during the war, and buried. Was his name ever known?"

There was a long pause. Gen. Garwood gazed steadily into the fire. His mother sighed gently. Hallie, who had been resting her head against Helen's shoulder, rose from her chair, and glided from the room as swiftly as a ghost.

"Perhaps I have made a mistake," said Helen in dismay. "The incident was so strange" —

"No, Miss Eustis, you have made no mistake," said Gen. Garwood, smiling a little sadly. "One moment" — He paused as if listening for something. Presently the faint sound of music was heard. It stole softly from the dark parlor into the warm firelight as if it came from far away.

"One moment," said Gen. Garwood. "It is Hallie at the piano."

The music, without increasing in volume, suddenly gathered coherency, and there fell on the ears of the listening group the notes of an air so plaintive that it seemed like the breaking of a heart. It was as soft as an echo, and as tender as the memories of love and youth.

"We have to be very particular with Hallie," said the general, by way of explanation. "The Union soldier in our burying-ground is intimately connected with her bereavement and ours. Hers is the one poor heart that keeps the fires of grief always burning. I think she is willing the story should be told."

"Yes," said his mother, "else she would never go to the piano."

"I feel like a criminal," said Helen. "How can I apologize?"

"It is we who ought to apologize and explain," replied Gen. Garwood. "You shall hear the story, and then neither explanation nor apology will be necessary."

VI.

A summons was sent for Uncle Prince, and the old man soon made his appearance. He stood in a seriously expectant attitude.

"Prince," said Gen. Garwood, "these ladies are from the North. They have asked me about the dead Union soldier you brought home during the war. I want you to tell the whole story."

"Tell 'bout de what, Marse Peyton?" Both astonishment and distress were depicted on the old negro's face as he asked the question. He seemed to be sure that he had not heard aright.

"About the Union soldier you brought home with your young master from Virginia."

"Whar Miss Hallie, Marse Peyton? Dat her in dar wid de peanner?"

"Yes, she's in there."

"I 'lowed she uz some'r's, kaze I know 'tain't gwine never do fer ter git dat chile riled up 'bout dem ole times; en it'll be a mighty wonder ef she don't ketch col' in dar whar she is."

"No," said Gen. Garwood; "the room is warm. There has been a fire in there all day."

"Yasser, I know I builted one in dar dis mornin', but I take notice dat de draffs dese times look like dey come bofe ways."

The old man stood near the tall mantel, facing the group. There was nothing servile in his attitude: on the contrary, his manner, when addressing the gentleman who had once been his master, suggested easy, not to say affectionate, familiarity. The fire-light, shining on his face, revealed a countenance at once rugged and friendly. It was a face in which humor had many a tough struggle with dignity. In looks and tone, in word and gesture, there was unmistakable evidence of that peculiar form of urbanity that cannot be dissociated from gentility. These things were more apparent, perhaps, to Helen and her aunt than to those who, from long association, had become accustomed to Uncle Prince's peculiarities.

"Dem times ain't never got clean out'n my min'," said the old negro, "but it bin so long sence I runn'd over um, dat I dunner wharbouts ter begin skacely."

"You can tell it all in your own way," said Gen. Garwood.

"Yasser, dat's so, but I fear'd it's a mighty po' way. Bless yo' soul, honey," Uncle Prince went on, "dey was rough times, en it look like ter me dat ef dey wuz ter come 'roun' ag'in hit 'u'd take a mighty rank runner fer ter ketch one nigger man w'at I'm got some 'quaintance wid. Dey wuz rough times, but dey wa'n't rough 'long at fust. Shoo! no! dey wuz dat slick dat dey ease we-all right down 'mongs' de wuss kind er tribbylation, en we ain't none un us know it twel we er done dar.

"I know dis," the old man continued, addressing himself exclusively to Miss Eustis and her aunt; "I knows dat we-all wuz a-gittin' 'long mighty well, w'en one day Marse Peyton dar, he tuck 'n' jinded wid de army; en den 'twa'n't long 'fo' word come dat my young marster w'at gwine ter college in Ferginny, done gone en jinded wid um. I ax myse'f, I say, w'at de name er goodness does dey want wid boy like dat? Hit's de Lord's trufe, ma'am, dat ar chile wa'n't mo' dan gwine on sixteen, ef he wuz dat, en I up'n' ax myse'f, I did, w'at does de war want wid baby like dat? Min' you, ma'am, I ain't fin' out den w'at war wuz — I ain't know w'at a great big maw she got."

"My son Ethel," said Mrs. Garwood, the soft tone of her voice chiming with the notes of the piano, "was attending the University of Virginia at Charlottesville. He was just sixteen."

"Yassum," said Uncle Prince, rubbing his hands together gently, and gazing into the glowing embers, as if searching there for some clew that would aid him in recalling the past. "Yassum, my young marster wuz des gone by sixteen year, kaze 'twa'n't so mighty long 'fo' dat, dat we-all sont 'im a great big box er fixin's en doin's fer ter git dar on he's birfday; en I sot up mighty nigh twel day tryin' ter make some 'lasses candy fer ter put in dar wid de yuther doin's."

Here Uncle Prince smiled broadly at the fire.

"Ef dey wuz sumpin' w'at dat chile like, hit wuz 'lasses candy; en I say ter my ole 'oman, I did, ''Mandy Jane, I'll make de candy, en den w'en she good en done, I'll up en holler fer you, en den you kin pull it.' Yassum, I said dem ve'y words. So de ole 'oman, she lay down 'cross de baid, en I sot up dar en b'iled de 'lasses. De 'lasses 'u'd blubber en I'd nod, en I'd nod en de 'lasses 'u'd blubber, en fus news I know de 'lasses 'u'd done be scorched. Well, ma'am, I tuck 'n' burnt up mighty nigh fo' gallons er 'lasses on de account er my noddin', en bimeby w'en de ole 'oman wake up, she 'low dey wa'n't no excusion fer it; en sho nuff dey wa'n't, kaze w'at make I nod dat away?

"But dat candy wuz candy, mon, w'en she did come, en den de ole 'oman she tuck 'n' pull it twel it git 'mos' right white; en my young marster, he tuck 'n' writ back, he did, dat ef dey wuz any thin' in dat box w'at make 'im git puny wid de homesickness, hit uz dat ar 'lasses candy. Yassum, he cert'n'y did, kaze dey tuck 'n' read it right out'n de letter whar he writ it.

"'Twa'n't long atter dat 'fo' we-all got de word dat

my young marster done jinded inter de war wid some
yuther boys w'at been at de same school'ouse wid
'im. Den, on top er dat, yer come news dat he gwine
git married. Bless yo' soul, honey, dat sorter rilded
me up, en I march inter de big 'ouse, I did, en I up
'n' tell mistis dat she better lemme go up dar en
fetch dat chile home; en den mistis say she gwine
sen' me on dar fer ter be wid 'im in de war, en take
keer un 'im. Dis holp me up might'ly, kaze I wuz
a mighty biggity nigger in dem days. De white
folks done raise me up right 'long wid um, en way
down in my min' I des laid off fer ter go up dar in
Ferginny, en take my young marster by he's collar
en fetch 'im home, des like I done w'en he use ter
git in de hin'ouse en bodder 'long wid de chickens.

"Dat wuz way down in my min', des like I tell
you, but bless yo' soul, chile, hit done drap out 'mos'
'fo' I git ter 'Gusty, in de Nunited State er Georgy.
Time I struck de railroad I kin see de troops a-troop-
in', en year de drums a-drummin'. De trains wuz
des loaded down wid um. Let 'lone de passenger
kyars, dey wuz in de freight-boxes yit, en dey wuz de
sassiest white mens dat yever walk 'pon topside de
groun'. Mon, dey wuz a caution. Dey had niggers
wid um, en de niggers wuz sassy, en ef I hadn't
a-frailed one un um out, I dunner w'at would er
'come un me.

"Hit cert'n'y wuz a mighty long ways fum dese
parts. I come down yer fum Ferginny in a waggin

w'en I wuz des 'bout big nuff fer ter hol' a plow
straight in de' furrer, but 'tain't look like ter me
dat 'twuz sech a fur ways. All day en all night long
fer mighty nigh a week I year dem kyar-wheels go
clickity-clock, clickity-clock, en dem ingines go choo-
choo-choo, choo-choo-choo, en it look like we ain't
never gwine git dar. Yit, git dar we did, en 'tain't
take me long fer ter fin' de place whar my young
marster is. I laid off ter fetch 'im home; well,
ma'am, w'en I look at 'im he skeer'd me. Yassum,
you may b'lieve me er not b'lieve me, but he skeer'd
me. Stiddier de boy w'at I wuz a-huntin' fer, dar he
wuz, a great big grow'd-up man, en bless yo' soul,
he wuz a-trompin' roun' dar wid great big boots on,
en, mon, dey had spurrers on um.

"Ef I hadn' er year 'im laugh, I nev'd a-know'd
'im in de roun' worl'. I say ter myse'f, s' I, I'll des
wait en see ef he know who I is. But shoo! my
young marster know me time he lays eyes on me, en
no sooner is he see me dan he fetched a whoop
en rushed at me. He 'low, 'Hello, Daddy! whar de
name er goodness you rise fum?' He allers call me
Daddy sence he been a baby. De minute he say
dat, it come over me 'bout how lonesome de folks
wuz at home, en I des grabbed 'im, en' low, 'Honey,
you better come go back wid Daddy.'

"He sorter hug me back, he did, en den he laugh,
but I tell you dey wa'n't no laugh in me, kaze I done
see w'iles I gwine long w'at kinder 'sturbance de

white folks wuz a-gittin' up, en I know'd dey wuz a-gwine ter be trouble pile 'pon trouble. Yit dar he wuz a-laughin' en a-projickin', en 'mongs' all dem yuther mens dey wa'n't none un um good-lookin' like my young marster. I don't keer w'at kinder cloze he put on, dey fit 'im, en I don't keer w'at crowd he git in, dey ain't none un um look like 'im. En 'tain't on'y me say dat; I done year lots er yuther folks say dem ve'y words.

"I ups en sez, s' I, 'Honey, you go 'long en git yo' things, en come go home 'long wid Daddy. Dey er waitin' fer you down dar,' — des so! Den he look at me cute like he us'ter w'en he wuz a baby, en he 'low, he did, —

"'I'm mighty glad you come, Daddy, en I hope you brung yo' good cloze, kaze you des come in time fer ter go in 'ten'ance on my weddin'.' Den I 'low, "'You oughtn' be a-talkin' dat away, honey. W'at in de name er goodness is chilluns like you got ter do wid marryin'?' Wid dat, he up 'n' laugh, but 'twa'n't no laughin' matter wid me. Yit 'twuz des like he tell me, en 'twa'n't many hours 'fo' we wuz gallopin' cross de country to'ds Marse Randolph Herndon' place; en dar whar he married. En you may b'lieve me er not, ma'am, des ez you please, but dat couple wuz two er de purtiest chilluns you ever laid eyes on, en dar Miss Hallie in dar now fer ter show you I'm a-tellin' de true word. 'Mos' 'fo' de weddin' wuz over, news come dat my young marster en de folks wid 'im mus' go back ter camps, en back we went.

"Well, ma'am, dar we wuz — a mighty far ways fum home, Miss Hallie a-cryin', en de war gwine on des same ez ef 'twuz right out dar in de yard. My young marster 'low dat I des come in time, kaze he mighty nigh pe'sh'd fer sumpin' 'n'er good ter eat. I whirled in, I did, en I cook 'im some er de right kinder vittles; but all de time I cookin', I say ter myse'f, I did, dat I mought er come too soon, er I mought er come too late, but I be bless' ef I come des in time.

"Hit went on dis away scan'lous. We marched en we stopped, en we stopped en we marched, en 'twuz de Lord's blessin' dat we rid hosses, kaze ef my young marster had 'a' bin 'blige' ter tromp thoo de mud like some er dem white mens, I speck I'd 'a' had ter tote 'im, dough he uz mighty spry en tough. Sometimes dem ar bung-shells 'u'd drap right in 'mongs' whar we-all wuz, en dem wuz de times w'en I feel like I better go off some'r's en hide, not dat I wuz anyways skeery, kaze I wa'n't; but ef one er dem ur bung-shells had er strucken me, I dunner who my young marster would 'a' got ter do he's cookin' en he's washin'.

"Hit went on dis away, twel bimeby one night, way in de night, my young marster come whar I wuz layin', en shuck me by de shoulder. I wuz des wide 'wake ez w'at he wuz, yit I ain't make no motion.

He shuck me ag'in, en 'low, 'Daddy! O Daddy! I'm gwine on de skirmish line. I speck we gwine ter have some fun out dar.'

"I 'low, I did, 'Honey, you make 'aste back ter break'us, kaze I got some sossige meat en some gennywine coffee."

"He ain't say nothin', but w'en he git little ways off, he tu'n 'roun' en come back, he did, en 'low, 'Good-night, Daddy.' I lay dar, en I year un w'en dey start off. I year der hosses a-snortin', en der spurrers a-jinglin'. Ef dey yever wuz a restless creetur hit uz me dat night. I des lay dar wid my eyes right wide open, en dey staid open, kaze, atter w'ile, yer come daylight, en den I rousted out, I did, en built me a fire, en 'twa'n't long 'fo' I had break'us a-fryin' en de coffee a-b'ilin', kaze I spected my young marster eve'y minute; en he uz one er dese yer kinder folks w'at want he's coffee hot, en all de yuther vittles on de jump.

"I wait en I wait, en still he ain't come. Hit cert'n'y look like a mighty long time w'at he stay 'way; en bimeby I tuck myse'f off ter make some inquirements, kaze mighty nigh all he's comp'ny done gone wid 'im. I notice dat de white mens look at me mighty kuse w'en I ax um 'bout my young marster; en bimeby one un um up en 'low, 'Ole man, whar yo' hat?' des dat away. I feel on my haid, en, bless goodness! my hat done gone; but I 'spon' back, I did, ''Tain't no time fer no nigger

man fer ter be bodder'n' 'bout he's hat,' des so.
Well, ma'am, bimeby I struck up wid some er my
young marster' comp'ny, en dey up 'n' tell me dat
dey had a racket out dar en de skirmish line, en dey
hatter run in, en dey speck my young marster be
'long terreckerly. Den I year some un say dat dey
speck de Yankees tuck some pris'ners out dar, en
den I know dat ain't gwine do fer me. I des runn'd
back ter whar we been campin', en I mount de hoss
w'at my young marster gun me, en I rid right
straight out ter whar dey been fightin'. My min'
tol' me dey wuz sumpin' 'n'er wrong out dar, en I
let you know, ma'am, I rid mighty fas'; I sholy
made dat ole hoss git up fum dar. De white mens
dey holler at me w'en I pass, but eve'y time dey
holler I make dat creetur men' he's gait. Some un
um call me a country-ban', en say I runnin' 'way, en
ef de pickets hadn't all been runnin' in, I speck dey'd
'a' fetched de ole nigger up wid de guns. But dat
never cross my min' dat day.

"Well, ma'am, I haid my hoss de way de pickets
comin' fum; en ef dey hadn't er been so much
underbresh en so many sassyfac saplin's, I speck I'd
'a' run dat creetur ter def: but I got ter whar I
hatter go slow, en I des pick my way right straight
forrerd de bes' I kin. I ain't hatter go so mighty
fur, nudder, 'fo' I come 'cross de place whar dey had
de skirmish; en fum dat day ter dis I ain't never see
no lonesome place like dat. Dey wuz a cap yer, a

hat yander, en de groun' look like it wuz des strowed wid um. I stop en listen. Den I rid on a little ways, en den I stop en listen. Bimeby I year hoss whicker, en den de creetur w'at I'm a-ridin', he whicker back, en do des like he wanter go whar de t'er hoss is. I des gin 'im de rein; en de fus news I know, he trot right up ter de big black hoss w'at my young marster rid.

"I look little furder, I did, en I see folks lyin' on de groun'. Some wuz double' up, en some wuz layin' out straight. De win' blow de grass back'ards en forrerds, but dem sojer-men dey never move; en den I know dey wuz dead. I look closer; en dar 'pon de groun', 'mos' right at me, wuz my young marster layin' right by de side er one er dem Yankee mens. I jumped down, I did, en run ter whar he wuz; but he wuz done gone. My heart jump, my knees shuck, en my han' trimble; but I know I got ter git away fum dar. Hit look like at fus' dat him en dat Yankee man been fightin'; but bimeby I see whar my young marster bin crawl thoo de weeds en grass ter whar de Yankee man wuz layin'; en he had one arm un' de man' haid, en de ter han' wuz gripped on he's canteen. I fix it in my min', ma'am, dat my young marster year dat Yankee man holler fer water; en he des make out fer ter crawl whar he is, en dar I foun' um bofe.

"Dey wuz layin' close by a little farm road, en not so mighty fur off I year a chicken crowin'. I say ter myse'f dat sholy folks must be livin' whar dey chickens crowin'; en I tuck'n' mount my young marster's hoss, en right 'roun' de side er de hill I come 'cross a house. De folks wuz all gone; but dey wuz a two-hoss waggin in de lot en some gear in de barn, en I des loped back atter de yuther hoss, en 'mos' 'fo' you know it, I had dem creeturs hitch up: en I went en got my young marster en de Yankee man w'at wuz wid 'im, en I kyard um back ter de camps. I got um des in time, too, kase I ain't mo'n fairly start 'fo' I year big gun, *be-bang!* en den I know'd de Yankees mus' be a-comin' back. Den de bung-shells 'gun ter bus'; en I ax myse'f w'at dey shootin' at me fer, en I ain't never fin' out w'at make dey do it.

"Well, ma'am, w'en I git back ter camps, dar wuz Cunnel Tip Herndon, w'ich he wuz own br'er ter Miss Hallie. Maybe you been year tell er Marse Tip, ma'am; he cert'n'y wuz a mighty fine man. Marse Tip, he 'uz dar, en 'twa'n't long 'fo' Miss Hallie wuz dar, kaze she ain't live so mighty fur; en Miss Hallie say dat my young marster en de Yankee man mus' be brung home terge'er. So dey brung um."

Uncle Prince paused. His story was at an end. He stooped to stir the fire; and when he rose, his eyes were full of tears. Humble as he was, he could pay this tribute to the memory of the boy soldier whom he had nursed in sickness and in health. It was a stirring recital. Perhaps it is not so stirring

when transferred to paper. The earnestness, the
simplicity, the awkward fervor, the dramatic gestures,
the unique individuality of Uncle Prince, cannot be
reproduced ; but these things had a profound effect
on Miss Eustis and her aunt.

VII.

THROUGHOUT the narrative the piano had been
going, keeping, as it seemed, a weird accompaniment
to a tragic story. This also had its effect ; for, so
perfectly did the rhythm and sweep of the music
accord with the heart-rending conclusion, that Helen,
if her mind had been less pre-occupied with sympathy, would probably have traced the effect of it all
to a long series of rehearsals: in fact, such a suggestion did occur to her, but the thought perished
instantly in the presence of the unaffected simplicity
and the childlike earnestness which animated the
words of the old negro.

The long silence which ensued — for the piano
ceased, and Hallie nestled at Helen's side once more
— was broken by Gen. Garwood.

"We were never able to identify the Union soldier.
He had in his possession a part of a letter, and a
photograph of himself. These were in an inner
pocket. I judge that he knew he was to be sent
on a dangerous mission, and had left his papers and
whatever valuables he may have possessed behind

him. The little skirmish in which he fell was a surprise to both sides. A scouting party of perhaps a dozen Federal cavalrymen rode suddenly upon as many Confederate cavalrymen who had been detailed for special picket duty. There was a short, sharp fight, and then both sides scampered away. The next day the Federal army occupied the ground."

"It is a pity," said Helen, "that his identity should be so utterly lost."

"Hallie, my dear," said Mrs. Garwood, "would it trouble you too much to get the photograph of the Union soldier? If it is any trouble, my child" —

Hallie went swiftly out of the room, and returned almost immediately with the photograph, and handed it to Helen, who examined it as well as she could by the dim firelight.

"The face is an interesting one, as well as I can make out," said Helen, "and it has a strangely familiar look. He was very young."

She handed the picture to her aunt. Her face was very pale.

"I can't see by this light," said Miss Tewksbury. But Uncle Prince had already brought a lamp which he had been lighting. "Why, my dear," said Miss Tewksbury, in a tone of voice that suggested both awe and consternation, — "why, my dear, this is your brother Wendell!"

"Oh, aunt Harriet! I thought so — I was afraid so — but are you sure?"

"As sure as that I am sitting here."

Helen burst into tears. "Oh, why didn't I recognize him? How could I fail to know my darling
brother?" she cried.

Hallie rose from her low stool, and stood gazing
at Helen. Her face was pale as death, but in her
eyes gleamed the fire of long-suppressed grief and
passion. She seemed like one transformed. She
flung her white arms above her head, and exclaimed, —

"I knew it! I knew it! I knew that some poor
heart would find its long-lost treasure here. I have
felt it — I have dreamed it! Oh, I am so glad you
have found your brother!"

"Oh, but I should have known his picture," said
Helen.

"But, my dear child," said Miss Tewksbury, in a
matter-of-fact way, "there is every reason why you
should not have known it. This picture was taken
in Washington, and he never sent a copy of it home.
If he did, your father put it away among his papers.
You were not more than twelve years old when
Wendell went away."

"Perhaps if Hallie will get the fragment of letter," said Gen. Garwood to Miss Tewksbury, "it will
confirm your impression."

"Oh, it is no impression," replied Miss Tewksbury.
"I could not possibly be mistaken."

The fragment of letter, when produced, proved to

be in the handwriting of Charles Osborne Eustis;
and there was one sentence in it that was peculiarly
characteristic. "Remember, dear Wendell," it said,
"that the war is not urged against men ; it is against
an institution which the whole country, both North
and South, will be glad to rid itself of."

It would be difficult, under all the circumstances,
to describe Helen's thoughts. She was gratified —
she was more than gratified — at the unexpected
discovery, and she was grateful to those who had
cared for her brother's grave with such scrupulous
care. She felt more at home than ever. The last
barrier of sectional reserve (if it may be so termed)
was broken down, so far as she was concerned ; and
during the remainder of her stay, her true character
— her womanliness, her tenderness, her humor —
revealed itself to these watchful and sensitive South-
erners. Even Miss Tewksbury, who had the excuse
of age and long habit for her prejudices, showed the
qualities that made her friends love her. In the language of the little rector, who made a sermon out of
the matter, "all things became homogeneous through
the medium of sympathy and the knowledge of
mutual suffering."

In fact, every thing was so agreeable during the
visit of Helen and her aunt to Waverly, — a visit
that was prolonged many days beyond the limit they
had set, — that Uncle Prince remarked on it one
night to his wife.

"I'm a nigger man, 'Mandy Jane," said he, "but I got two eyes, en dey er good ones. W'at I sees I knows, en I tell you right now, Marse Peyton is done got strucken."

"Done got strucken 'bout what?" inquired 'Mandy Jane.

"'Bout dat young lady w'at stayin' yer. Oh, you neenter holler," said Uncle Prince in response to a contemptuous laugh from 'Mandy Jane. "I ain't nothin' but a nigger man, but I knows w'at I sees."

"Yes, you is a nigger man," said 'Mandy Jane triumphantly. "Ef you wuz a nigger 'oman you'd have lots mo' sense dan w'at you got. W'y, dat lady up dar ain't our folks. She mighty nice, I speck, but she ain't our folks. She ain't talk like our folks yit."

"No matter 'bout dat," said Uncle Prince. "I ain't seed no nicer 'oman dan w'at she is, en I boun' you she kin talk mighty sweet w'en she take a notion. W'en my two eyes tell me de news I knows it, en Marse Peyton done got strucken long wid dat white 'oman."

"En now you gwine tell me," said 'Mandy Jane with a fine assumption of scorn, "dat Marse Peyton gwine marry wid dat w'ite 'oman en trapse off dar ter der Norf? *Shoo!* Nigger man, you go ter bed 'fo' you run yo'se'f 'stracted."

"I dunno whar Marse Peyton gwine, 'Mandy Jane, but I done see 'im talkin' 'long wid dat white lady, en lookin' at her wid he's eyes. Huh! don' tell me!

En dat ain't all, 'Mandy Jane," Uncle Prince went on : "dat Bud Stucky, he's f'rever'n etarnally sneakin' 'roun' de house up dar. One day he want sumpin' ter eat, en nex' day he want Miss Hallie fer ter play en de peanner, but all de time I see 'im a-watchin' dat ar white lady fum de Norf."

"Hush !" exclaimed 'Mandy Jane.

"Des like I tell you !" said Uncle Prince.

"Well, de nasty, stinkin', oudacious villyun !" commented 'Mandy Jane. "I lay ef I go up dar en set de dogs on 'im, he'll stop sneakin' 'roun' dis place."

"Let 'im 'lone, 'Mandy Jane, let 'im 'lone," said Uncle Prince solemnly. "Dat ar Bud Stucky, he got a mammy, en my min' tell me dat he's mammy kin run de kyards en trick you. Now you watch out, 'Mandy Jane. You go on en do de washin', like you bin doin', en den ole Miss Stucky won't git atter you wid de kyards en cunjur you. Dat ole 'oman got er mighty bad eye, mon."

VIII.

UNCLE PRINCE, it appears, was a keen observer, especially where Gen. Garwood was concerned. He had discovered a fact in regard to "Marse Peyton," as he called him, that had only barely suggested itself to that gentleman's own mind, — the fact that his interest in Miss Eustis had assumed a phase altogether new and unexpected. Its manifestations

were pronounced enough to pester Miss Tewksbury,
but, strange to say, neither Gen. Garwood nor Miss
Eustis appeared to be troubled by them. As a matter of fact, these two were merely new characters
in a very old story, the details of which need not be
described or dwelt on in this hasty chronicle. It
was not by any means a case of love at first sight.
It was better than that : it was a case of love based
on a firmer foundation than whim, or passion, or sen-
timentality. At any rate, Helen and her stalwart
lover were as happy, apparently, as if they had just
begun to enjoy life and the delights thereof. There
was no love-making, so far as Miss Tewksbury could
see ; but there was no attempt on the part of either
to conceal the fact that they heartily enjoyed each
other's companionship.

Bud Stucky continued his daily visits for several
weeks ; but one day he failed to make his appearance, and after a while news came that he was ill
of a fever. The ladies at Waverly sent his mother
a plentiful supply of provisions, together with such
delicacies as seemed to them necessary ; but Bud
Stucky continued to waste away. One day Helen,
in spite of the protests of her aunt, set out to visit
the sick man, carrying a small basket in which Hallie
had placed some broiled chicken and a small bottle
of home-made wine. Approaching the Stucky cabin,
she was alarmed at the silence that reigned within.
She knocked, but there was no response ; whereupon

she pushed the door open and entered. The sight that met her eyes, and the scene that followed, are still fresh in her memory.

Poor Bud Stucky, the shadow of his former self, was lying on the bed. His thin hands were crossed on his breast, and the pallor of death was on his emaciated face. His mother sat by the bed with her eyes fixed on his. She made no sign when Helen entered, but continued to gaze on her son. The young woman, bent on a mission of mercy, paused on the threshold, and regarded the two unfortunates with a sympathy akin to awe. Bud Stucky moved his head uneasily, and essayed to speak; but the sound died away in his throat. He made another effort. His lips moved feebly; his voice had an unearthly, a far-away sound.

"Miss," he said, regarding her with a piteous expression in his sunken eyes, "I wish you'd please, ma'am, make maw let me go." He seemed to gather strength as he went on. "I'm all ready, an' a-waitin'; I wish you'd please, ma'am, make 'er let me go."

"Oh, what can I do?" cried Helen, seized with a new sense of the pathos that is a part of the humblest human life.

"Please, ma'am, make 'er let me go. I been a-layin' here ready two whole days an' three long nights, but maw keeps on a-watchin' of me; she won't let me go. She's got 'er eyes nailed on me constant."

Helen looked at the mother, Her form was wasted by long vigils, but she sat bolt upright in her chair, and in her eyes burned the fires of an indomitable will. She kept them fixed on her son. "Won't you please, ma'am, tell maw to let me go? I'm so tired er waitin'." The plaintive voice seemed to be an echo from the valley of the shadow of death. Helen, watching narrowly and with agonized curiosity, thought she saw the mother's lips move; but no sound issued therefrom. The dying man made another appeal : — "Oh, I'm so tired! I'm all ready, an' she won't let me go. A long time ago when I us' ter ax 'er, she'd let me do 'most any thing, an' now she won't let me go. Oh, Lordy! I'm so tired er waitin'! Please, ma'am, ax 'er to let me go."

Mrs. Stucky rose from her chair, raised her clasped hands above her head, and turned her face away. As she did so, something like a sigh of relief escaped from her son. He closed his eyes, and over his wan face spread the repose and perfect peace of death.

Turning again towards the bed, Mrs. Stucky saw Helen weeping gently. She gazed at her a moment. "Whatter you cryin' fer now?" she asked with unmistakable bitterness. "You wouldn't a-wiped your feet on 'im. Ef you wuz gwine ter cry, whyn't you let 'im see you do it 'fore he died? What good do it do 'im now? He wa'n't made out'n i'on like me."

Helen made no reply. She placed her basket on

the floor, went out into the sunlight, and made her way swiftly back to Waverly. Her day's experience made a profound impression on her, so much so that when the time came for her to go home, she insisted on going alone to bid Mrs. Stucky good-by.

She found the lonely old woman sitting on her door-sill. She appeared to be gazing on the ground, but her sun bonnet hid her face. Helen approached, and spoke to her. She gave a quick upward glance, and fell to trembling. She was no longer made of iron. Sorrow had dimmed the fire of her eyes. Helen explained her visit, shook hands with her, and was going away, when the old woman, in a broken voice, called her to stop. Near the pine-pole gate was a little contrivance of boards that looked like a bird-trap. Mrs. Stucky went to this, and lifted it.

"Come yer, honey," she cried, "yer's somepin' I wanter show you." Looking closely, Helen saw moulded in the soil the semblance of a footprint. "Look at it, honey, look at it," said Mrs. Stucky; "that's his darlin' precious track."

Helen turned, and went away weeping. The sight of that strange memorial, which the poor mother had made her shrine, leavened the girl's whole after-life.

When Helen and her aunt came to take their leave of Azalia, their going away was not by any means in the nature of a merry-making. They went away sorrowfully, and left many sorrowful friends behind them. Even William, the bell-ringer and

purveyor of hot batter-cakes at Mrs. Haley's hotel,
walked to the railroad-station to see them safely
off. Gen. Garwood accompanied them to Atlanta;
and though the passenger-depot in that pushing city
is perhaps the most unromantic spot to be found in
the wide world, — it is known as the "Car-shed" in
Atlantese, — it was there that he found courage to
inform Miss Eustis that he purposed to visit Boston
during the summer in search not only of health, but
of happiness; and Miss Eustis admitted, with a reserve both natural and proper, that she would be
very happy to see him.

It is not the purpose of this chronicle to follow
Gen. Garwood to Boston. The files of the Boston
papers will show that he went there, and that, in a
quiet way, he was the object of considerable social
attention. But it is in the files of the "Brookline
Reporter" that the longest and most graphic account
of the marriage of Miss Eustis to Gen. Garwood is
to be found. It is an open secret in the literary
circles of Boston, that the notice in the "Reporter"
was from the pen of Henry P. Bassett, the novelist.
It was headed "Practical Reconstruction;" and it was
conceded on all sides, that, even if the article had
gone no farther than the head-line, it would have
been a very happy description of the happiest of
events.